BLAKE'S COME HOME

SUSSAN LAWES

Integrity Publishing
39343 Harbor Hills Blvd Lady Lake,
FL 32159

www.integrity-publishing.com

CHAPTER 1

BLAKE WAS BONE tired; he'd been travelling for nearly eighteen hours all he wanted was a soothing hot shower and twelve hours of uninterrupted sleep.

He knew there would be no chance of that until he'd seen his Mother and that was better done sooner than later.

It had been over five years since he's been back to his home town. He cringed inside thinking of his life in those times. He was a lost soul not knowing where his future lay.

His Mother was pressuring him into joining the family Company, an engineering firm his Father had built from scratch into one of the biggest Industrial Companies in the country. Then there was his wife Mickie, all she ever wanted was to be his wife and the mother of his children. She put his happiness before her own but even that wasn't enough to keep him here, he ran as fast and as far as he could from everything and everyone he cared about.

The one regret he had was leaving Mickie behind; he knew she would have followed him to the ends of the earth as long as they were together. Her love and unshakeable belief in him weighed so heavy on his shoulders at that time, he could feel the walls caving in around him. He felt like a failure and he didn't want to see the disappointment in her eyes, so like a coward he walked away. Blake still suffered guilt remembering the way he just packed his bags and walked out, he wasn't even man enough to face her just left her a note to explain it all.

He realized his mistake in leaving her behind in the first couple of months and tried to call her repeatedly over those weeks, eventually he asked his mother to go and see her, ask her to contact him. Cybil informed him that Mickie had sold the house and moved away not leaving a forwarding address.

The taxi pulled up in front of his parent's palatial home and by the looks of it his Mother was having one of her dinner parties, great that was all he needed. His Mother would make a fuss in front of all her snooty friends and he was too damn tired to deal with it all now. Wearily he paid the cab fare, reaching for his bags he headed towards the front door, he rang the door bell. While waiting for it to be answered he wondered if Dotty, his Mother's maid was still working for her, hearing the door open he was pleasantly surprised to see the subject of his musing standing before him. She hadn't aged a day; he knew she must be close to eighty and wondered why she hadn't retired yet.

"Well I'll be, if it ain't Master Blake. Never thought I'd see your pretty face around these parts again seein' the way you high tailed it outta here all those years ago." Even though she smiled he could hear the admonishment in her voice.

"Life's full of surprises Dotty." He said with a tired smile as he gave the woman that had been like a mother to him a hug.

"How have you been Dotty, thought you would have retired by now and be enjoying your grandchildren."

Dotty huffed, "What would your mother do without me? She scares the daylights out of all the other girls, so she needs me to keep this house running smoothly." She replied as she returned his embrace lovingly. She looked up into the face of the boy she affectionately thought of as a son, she could see he was dead on his feet.

She ushered him into the foyer, "Did your Ma now you were coming tonight?"

Blake shook his head.

"I didn't think so or she wouldn't have invited all them fancy folk over."

Blake smile, Dotty had no time for people who thought they were better than everyone else just because they had money.

Mother's friends had a tendency to treat those less fortunate with distain and Dotty would have none of it, if they spoke to her disrespectfully she would give them both barrels. Dotty treated everyone as equal's rich or poor, the only one that she did treat differently was Mickie and she held a special place in Dotty's heart.

"Do you think I might be able to sneak upstairs and grab a shower and a couple of hours sleep before I face my Mother?"

The pleading look in his eyes would soften the hardest of hearts and where Blake was concerned Dotty always had a very soft spot just for him.

"Of course but get a wiggle on cause if your Ma catches us we'll both get a lashing from that nasty tongue of hers."

She reached down to pick up his bag following him up to his room, once there he made a bee line for the shower stripping off his clothes as he went. Dotty smiled, just like old times it was good to have him home. Dotty pulled back the covers on the bed; she wondered what had bought him home, whatever it was she hoped it had a better outcome than before. She closed the door on the way out making her way to the kitchen to make coffees for Cybil's guests.

CHAPTER 2

IN A COTTAGE on the other side of town, Mickie and Dylan were watching the latest animated movie on DVD when the phone rang; reaching behind Dylan she answered it.

Listening to the caller she lost all color in her face, the knuckles on her hand went white with the pressure in which she was squeezing the receiver.

She couldn't believe what she was hearing. No, not after all this time, not now that she had finally come to terms with the fact he was never coming back. Blake Hunter had come home.

Mickie thanked the caller and hung up the phone; Dylan looked over at his Mother and sensed something was wrong.

"Mummy, you ok?" he asked

When she didn't answer he became more worried, tugging on her sleeve, "Mummy what's wrong, it's not Grampa is it?

Dylan's question finally penetrated her thoughts; glancing down at the exact replica of his father she answered him.

"No sweetheart that wasn't about Grampa it was Aunty Dotty."

Changing the subject she asked how he liked the movie.

"It's great Mum can we hire it again when Danny comes over?"

Danny was Dylan's best friend.

"Sure Honey, how about a hot chocolate before you go to bed?" "Okay." Dylan's attention went back to the movie as Mickie got up and headed for the kitchen to make the drinks.

As she waited for the milk to heat her mind drifted to Blake.

She had thought she was over him bit just the mention of his name and her tummy fluttered, she wasn't sure if it was from anger, hurt or something else. They say time heals all wounds but it was obvious not enough time had passed for her to forget Blake.

Drinks made Mickie carried them back to the lounge just as the movie was finishing, she handed Dylan his.

"Honey, when you've finished hop upstairs and get ready for bed, I'll be up shortly to tuck you in."

"Ok Mummy. Can I wear my new jamas?"

"Sure Baby, just put your others in the wash."

While Dylan was getting ready for bed Mickie washed the cups and headed upstairs for a quick shower, after tucking her son in for the night she climbed into her bed, pulling up the covers, she stared at the ceiling remembering the day her world fell apart. The day Blake left her.

CHAPTER 3

MICKIE LITERALLY FLOATED out of the doctor's office, she was happier than she ever thought possible, she couldn't wait to get home and tell Blake her news she knew he would be as ecstatic as she was, they had wanted this for so long.

They had been married for just over two years much to Cybil's, Blake's Mother's disgust. She had been against their marriage from the start, Mickie wasn't good enough for the "Hunter Family", came from the wrong side of the tracks and worst of all had no money. Despite Cybil's numerous attempts to sabotage Mickie and Blake's relationship they did marry. Mickie's father George was as proud as any father could be as he walked his beautiful daughter down the aisle, there were tears in his eyes as he handed her over to the man he already considered a son. They had been so much in love then, the world was their oyster. After a two week honeymoon they settled into married life, moving into the house Blake's parents had bought them as a wedding present.

Blake and one of his buddies from University started up a computer software company. Blake wrote programs for all sorts of things and Steve would sell them to organizations and companies. This upset Cybil; she wanted Blake to join 'Hunter Engineering', the family business, Blake's father was proud that his son wanted to do something of his own. He would often tell Cybil to leave Blake alone, that a man needed to find his own way and the business would always be there if Blake changed his mind. Richard admired Blake for starting out on his own and not relying on his family's money but then Blake was never like that. From an early age he was earning his own money from mowing lawns, doing a paper round, delivering pamphlet, Mickie suspected he did it all to get away from his mother.

Mickie often wondered why Richard had married Cybil, they were complete opposites. He was easy going, affectionate, loving and generous, sometimes to a fault. Richard never judged a person by their wealth; he treated everyone as equals unlike Cybil. She was cold and calculating only associating with the affluent of the community. Mickie couldn't remember a single moment where Cybil display any form of affection all she ever saw from her was disapproval, anger and spite. Cybil loved to humiliate Mickie in front of her exalted friends and did it at every opportunity. She would parade her friend's beautiful eligible daughters in front of Blake in hope one of them would lure him away from Mickie. One that Cybil was constantly throwing at Blake on a regular basis was Olivia James. Olivia had gone to school with Mickie; they had never been friends as she always hung around with girls of similar standing, still Olivia had been jealous of Mickie throughout their school years. It was something Mickie could never understand as Olivia was beautiful in her own right. To get at Mickie she would sleep with any guy that showed the slightest bit of interest in her. Olivia had boys running around her like moths to a flame, the only one that showed no interest in her at all was Blake; he only had eyes for Mickie. Olivia tried everything she could think of to get Blake but to no avail. Cybil knew of Olivia's hatred of Mickie and her love for Blake and would constantly orchestrate her being at the same social events. That's when Blake would get angry with her and they would have a huge fight, Cybil would scream hysterically at Blake that he was wasting his life with a tramp like Mickie, at those times Mickie thought Cybil tread a very thin line between sanity and insanity. Mickie loved it then, as Blake would refuse to see or talk to his Mother Mickie knew it was to punish Cybil for the way she treated her, sometimes they could go months without contact, those were happy times.

One fight that stuck in Mickie's mind; happened a couple of months before Blake walked out. They had been attending another of Cybil's charitable events, this one for disadvantaged children. There were hundreds of people from the community there and Cybil seemed at her worst that night. She stood on stage in front of the crowd and told them that her family had been supporting disadvantaged children for many years even to the point that her son had married one. A collective hush crossed the room, all heads turned towards Blake and Mickie. Richard stormed up onto the stage and took his wife aside; he was disgusted in her, he reprimanded her for using such a forum to humiliate not just Mickie but the whole family including herself, Cybil couldn't see that she had done anything wrong.

Mickie had never seen Blake so angry; grabbing her hand he approached his Mother. He told her he never wanted to see or speak to her again, when Olivia stepped in front of him telling him this wouldn't have happened if he hadn't married Mickie. Blake turned on Olivia telling her she was nothing but his Mother's whore selling herself to the highest bidder and if she was the last woman on earth he wouldn't touch her with a barge pole. All this played out in front of the whole town. Mickie had never been so embarrassed;

everyone knew of Cybil's hatred towards her daughter-in-law but this was the first time Cybil had stated it so publicly.

Cybil tried for weeks to speak to Blake, would show up at his office only to be turn away by Steve, even though Mickie hated how Cybil treated her she tried to talk Blake around. Family meant the world to Mickie and it hurt to see Blake estranged from his Mother even though she deserved it. Looking back Mickie realized it had been a mistake for him to reconcile with Cybil, especially with the outcome from the day Blake left.

CHAPTER 4

MICKIE HAD GONE shopping after leaving the doctor's office, she was so excited, she would cook Blake his favorite dinner, they would snuggle up on the sofa and she would give him the little blue bear she'd bought and tell him they were finally going to become parents.

As soon as she got home she headed for the kitchen and started preparing the evening meal, when everything was ready she headed for the shower.

She missed seeing the white envelope propped on the pillow as she hurried around the room getting ready for when Blake came home, she was so excited she could have burst. It was while she was putting the finishing touches to her makeup she spotted the note on her pillow, she smiled lovingly; Blake often left her notes around the house telling her how much he loved her. She rushed over and tore it open, slowly she lowered herself onto the bed as she read.

> *My Darling Mickie,*
> *Please forgive me for not saying this in person; if I had to face you I doubt I would have been able to say the words.*
> *Things haven't been right with me for a while now, I know I should have said something to you but you have been having your own problems and I didn't want to add to your burden.*

I struggle daily just to get up out of bed and go to work, all I want to do is pull the covers over my head and stay there forever. Knowing this I feel I have to get away, be on my own for a while.

Please believe that I love you with all my heart and I hate like hell to hurt you, but I am slowly dying inside a little every day.

The pressures from work and the constant dramas from my Mother have taken their toll. I know you must think me a coward for leaving and not facing my problems but they have become too much for me.

The pressure my Mother is putting on me to join Dad's company, her constant attacks on you especially the other week and doing it so publicly and I know how desperately you want a baby, but right now deep down inside I know that I wouldn't be able to take on being a father as well everything else.

If I stay I know I will make your life as miserable as I am making my own and eventually you would grow to hate me and that is something that I could never live with.

I hope you can forgive me for the hurt I am causing you.

My leaving has nothing to do with you, it's just me. You are the only decent thing I have in my life, you've kept me sane but I know I can't make you responsible for my happiness.

I need time to get my head sorted out and when I do I will contact you and if you still want me we could have a life together away from Lawson.

Please remember that I will always love you no matter what happens there will be never be other woman for me but you.

I do Love you Mickie with all my heart, never forget that.

Forever yours
Blake xxx

Tears streamed down Mickie's face, thoughts were bombarding her head, what were the problems Blake was having, was he alright?

Why was this happening now when everything was so right? She thought back over the weeks and Blake did seem preoccupied a lot of the time but she thought it had to do with the defense program he had been writing, she never realized it was his personal life that was causing him so much pain.

While Mickie was trying to come to grips that her husband had left her, Cybil used her key to enter the house. She went storming through the house room by room calling out for Mickie, finding her in the master bedroom Cybil tore into Mickie screaming abuse at her.

Halfway through her barrage she realized Mickie was taking no notice of her, years of pent up anger and jealousy caused Cybil to lash out and strike at Mickie. She'd hit her several times scratching her cheek and drawing blood before Mickie snapped out of her shock, ducking her head just in time to miss another blow from Cybil.

"Finally got your attention," Cybil spat at her. "I want you out of this house by morning and take all your trash with you anything you leave behind you can collect from the dump." Cybil took another swipe at Mickie missing her face by mere millimeters.

Mickie's mouth gaped open, "You can't order me out of my own home, are you crazy?"

Cybil laughed, "This was never your home, this is Blake's home and I see he has finally come to his senses and left you, I knew he would." Cybil stopped pacing in front of the bed, pointing a manicured finger in her face. "People like you make me sick thinking they can marry into a family like the 'Hunters', our breeding is of the highest quality while yours is lower than pond scum. You are nothing but a money grabbing little harlot and I can guarantee you my next daughter-in-law will have the appropriate credentials fit for this family." With that parting shot she walked out of the room, "Remember be out by morning."

Mickie couldn't believe this was happening; she rushed to the bathroom and emptied the contents of her stomach, rinsing her mouth she picked up the phone and called her father, as she waited for his arrival she curled up into a ball and wept.

CHAPTER 5

Aᴅɪꜱᴄʀᴇᴇᴛ ᴋɴᴏᴄᴋ aroused Blake from his sleep, rubbing his eyes he called, "Come in."

Dotty entered the room, he was half expecting it to be his Mother, and walked toward the bed with a breakfast tray. Shimming up the bed Blake folded the sheet discreetly over his lap, she handed him the tray, "Thank you Dotty, you didn't have to do this," Looking at the breakfast in front of him he smiled, "And it's my favorite crumpets with honey," he took a swig of his coffee, "And coffee just as I like it, hot and strong."

"I know that's why you got it," she opened the curtains to let in the morning sunlight. Smiling she said, "I thought you might like to face your Mother on a full stomach. You know she will be furious with you for not telling her you were coming home."

"Yeah, I know, maybe you should have bought me a bottle of scotch instead of coffee," he said as he took a mouthful of the hot brew.

She laughed, "Like that would help."

Leaving him to his breakfast Dotty closed the door behind her.

Blake finished his meal, grabbed some clothes and headed for the shower.

Cybil looked up from reading the society section of the paper when the dining room door opened, her face lit up when she saw Blake standing there.

"Darling you never said you were coming home, have you just arrived? Come and sit here," She patted the seat next to her.

"How was your trip?"

Blake greeted his parents, "Hello Mother, Dad."

Richard's "Blake" was said behind his morning paper.

Blake looked at his Mother a little confused; it appeared his Father wasn't as overjoyed to have him back home.

Cybil chastised Richard, "Richard, you could at least look at your only son when you speak to him, he has finally come home to us after such a long time away."

Richard laid his paper on the table, rose and for the first time in five years looked at his son, "It's good to see you home Blake. Are you staying long?"

Cybil's, "Richard really, he's only just walked in the house of course he's staying."

Turning to Blake she said, "Ignore your Father he obviously got out of the wrong side of the bed."

Blake looked over at his Father; he definitely wasn't feeling the love. "To answer your question yes I will be here for a while there's a few things I need to see to."

Richard walked to the door turning, he said, "I'll see you later." He then left the room. Richard wondered why after all this time had Blake come home, he needed to get to Mickie's and let her know.

Cybil rushed into speech trying to make up for Richard's bizarre behaviour. "It's good to have you home Darling, tell me what you've been up to? How's your business going? I'm so proud of your success, it seems your leaving here was the best thing you could have done. Now that you have divorced that scheming little witch we should see about getting you a proper wife."

Blake was only half listening to his Mother's ramblings but her mention of Mickie in such derogative terms caught his attention.

"Mother you know exactly what's been going on, you sent that private investigator to keep tabs on me."

Cybil didn't deny it, "Well what did you expect? You cut off all communication I just wanted to make sure you were okay."

"Sure Mother, and by the way you can forget about finding me another wife, I intend to find out what happened to Mickie and if she will forgive me, I intend to ask her to a marry me."

Blake didn't think it was at all possible but he had left his Mother speechless and gapping like a fish out of water.

When she finally found her voice it bellowed throughout the room, "Like hell you will. I will not allow you to embarrass this family again by associating with that bitch, you hear me. Anyway you finally saw her for what she was, a money grabbing little whore that's why you left."

Blake raised his eyebrows, "You won't allow me to do what, Mother!" His voice dropped an octave. "I'm not the person who stood up in front of the whole town and embarrassed and humiliated this family. And when did I EVER need to ask your permission to marry." He was really angry now. "Be very careful Mother because the next time I leave I will make it permanent and let me set the record straight, I didn't leave because of Mickie, in fact you were one of the main reasons that I left." Cybil gasped, but Blake continued, "Unfortunately I left the best thing in my life behind and I now intend to rectify that."

Blake could feel his temper raising; he never could understand his Mother's animosity towards his wife. Mickie had never once said a bad word against her even though she had every right considering the treatment she had received from his acid tongued Mother.

"So Mother did you actually check to see if Mickie was at the house at all, how much effort was put in looking for Mickie?"

One look at his Mother's face Blake realized she had done nothing to contact Mickie. "I should have known better than to trust you. I should have got Steve to do it, be warned Mother if I find you had anything to do with her leaving town I will make you pay dearly." Blake's threat was coming through as clear as crystal, Cybil started getting very nervous. Her son had changed and not for the better it would seem, before he would listen to her except when it came to that woman. She felt sure she had covered any tracks that would lead back to her. Looking at her son, he seemed harder somehow, she needed to change the subject and get his mind off that woman.

"Darling let's not fight on your first day back, I'd like organize a little get together with some of our friends to celebrate your return."

"Mother I don't want a party." Blake knew exactly where this was going.

"Don't be silly, there will just be a few people over to welcome you back that's all, I'll organize it for tomorrow night; if you wish to invite anyone just let me know the numbers. Oh by the way Olivia James came back to town a month ago seems her marriage has ended as well. You two will have something in common, I always thought you looked good together, maybe something will come of that now."

There is was, he knew she couldn't help herself, "Sorry to disappoint you Mother but Olivia and I have nothing in common; in fact I detest the woman, so if that was your plan you can forget it. There is only one woman I want and no matter how many of your friend's daughters you parade in front of me, "I'M NOT INTERESTED!"

Irritated Cybil snapped, "Blake a person should learn from their mistakes, not keep repeating them."

He needed to know why, "Mother, why do you hate her so much?"

"Because she thought she could just waltz in and marry someone of our standing and become one of us. You confused sex with love and instead of just sleeping with her or keeping her as your mistress you went and married the little gold digger."

Blake shook his head, "I feel sorry for you, Mother, you obviously don't know what love is. The love I have for Mickie will never end and if I never find her I will still love her to the day I die nothing will ever change that. If by chance I do find someone else I will never love them as I do her."

This angered Cybil; she did know what love was, she still held a special place in her heart for the love of her life but one had to make sacrifices as she had done. She would not let that woman have that kind of hold over Blake she should have gotten rid of her permanently the first time. She would just have to make sure Olivia crossed Blake's path on a regular basis she would soon make him forget that trollop.

The phone rang and his Mother was summoned to answer it.

That was his cue to leave as well, he had a few things he wanted to check, catch up with some old friends maybe they could give him some info on Mickie's whereabouts.

CHAPTER 6

THE DOORBELL RANG interrupting Mickie and Dylan's breakfast, as she rose to answer it she instructed DJ to finish his cereal.

Checking the peephole she saw the distorted features of her father-in-law, Richard. Releasing the deadlocks she admitted him into the foyer, he kissed her cheek in passing on the way to the Kitchen, the hub of the house. Dj looked up seeing his grandfather bounced off his chair leaping into Richard's welcoming arms.

"Hi Grampa," he said after delivering a milky kissed to Richards' cheek. "What cha doing here?"

Returning Dj's embrace and kissing the top of his head, Richard replied, "I've come to see my favourite grandson of course."

Dylan loved it when his grandfather came over, it was one of the times he would see his Mum laugh and smile a lot.

"You should a come earlier Grampa," Dylan scolded, "I havta go to kindy soon."

Mickie smiled as she watched the interaction between her son and his grandfather, he was apple of Richard's eye. Richard had supported Mickie while she was pregnant and would often sit with him while she was building her business.

Richard was openly affectionate towards Dj and the main male figure in his life, Dj adored his grandfather.

While her two favourite people caught up on the latest gossip Mickie brewed herself and Richard a cup of coffee, as she reached the kitchen table a car horn blasted from the driveway.

"That's Kathy," Dj informed his grandfather, he scooted off Richard's knee to collect his bag from the hallway, returning he kissed his grandfather goodbye and ran to the front door Mickie trailing behind.

Mickie greeted Kathy and Danny as she helped Dylan into his car seat, giving Dylan a kiss she said, "Now you be a good boy for Kathy and Mike and I'll pick you up Sunday afternoon."

Kathy laughed, "He's always a good boy, can't say the same for these others though, it's my lot that are unruly."

Dylan liked Kathy she was fun, she sometimes played cowboys and Indians with them and she would let them tie her to a chair so they could pretend to rescue her from the Indians.

Mickie wondered how Kathy did it with three boys, she found one a handful.

She waved them off and returned to the kitchen.

While Richard waited for Mickie to return he wondered what had bought Blake home, he hoped it wasn't to cause Mickie anymore heartache.

He remembered the day he got the phone call he from his best friend George Sullivan, Mickie's father. George was furious. Mickie had just called him saying Cybil had attacked her and ordered her out of the house. Richard had left work immediately to meet George at Mickie and Blake's house.

On his way over he knew he would have to do something about his wife, she was becoming more unstable every day and anything to do with Mickie sent her into a screaming banshee, he would look into getting her checked out after he sorted out other one of her messes.

When he arrived at Mickie's George was showing the doctor out, worried he asked, "Is Mickie alright, where's Blake?"

George closed the door, "Yes her fine just in shock, that bitch of a wife of yours did a number on Mickie's face and your son has left Mickie."

Richard was gobbed smacked, "What the hell is going with this family, can I see her?"

"Sure, the doc gave her a sedative so she will be a bit groggy."

Richard entered the bedroom Mickie was laying on the bed with a blanket over her; he knelt next to the bed, "Hey Sweetheart, are you ok?"

Tears ran down her nail scored cheek, Richard was furious Cybil would pay for her attack on Mickie.

She nodded, "Rick why did he leave me? If he didn't want a baby he only had to tell me."

Richard looked towards George, his friend shrugged his shoulders.

He turned once more to Mickie, "Honey, are you pregnant?"

Mickie nodded, "Blake doesn't want babies, that's why he's left me." Mickie's eyes fluttered closed the sedative was taking effect.

Standing Richard dragged his hand through his hair; George motioned him to step out of the room. They went to the kitchen where George put the kettle on.

"Christ George, do you know what's going on?"

George handed him Blake's note, he made the coffee as Richard read Blake's letter. When he finished George explained the rest.

"Seems Cybil tried to get hold of Blake at work and they told her he had quit and was moving interstate. She came storming over here trying to catch him but he had already left so I guess she took her anger out on Mickie. Mickie said she hit her several times and obviously raked her nails down her face to get her attention. Cybil then ordered Mickie out of the house by the morning or she would see her stuff dumped at the refuse centre.

I've got to tell you Rick, if I come face to face with that witch of a woman I swear I will strangle the life out of her. She has accused my little girl of some horrendous things and caused her a lot of grief over the years but this tops the cake. I am getting a restraining order put against her in the morning and if she comes anywhere near my baby I'll have her arrested.

Richard was stunned, he knew Cybil could be a real bitch at times but this was going way too far even for her. "Make sure you do it, it will take the wind out of her sails and it will cause her a huge embarrassment amongst her friends. She needs to know there are consequences to such actions and be reminded that she is not above the law. Don't worry about Mickie leaving here, this is her home for as long as she wants, I'll sort Cybil out. Did you know that Mickie was pregnant?"

George shook his head, "No that was as much as a surprise to me as it was to you." He laughed, "We're going to become Grand Pappies Rick."

Rick smiled, "I can't believe it. Will the baby be alright do you think?"

"I'll take her to the doctors in the morning and have her checked over, but it is only early days." George assured him.

Mickie slept for several hours, waking she went looking for her father she found him and Rick in the lounge, "Dad, Rick?"

Both men jumped up to help her to the sofa, her face pale except for the three large welts that seemed to dominate her cheeks.

Concerned the both asked, "Are you ok Sweetheart?"

Tears filled her eyes it tore a both men's hearts to see her like this, looking at them both she said, "Why did he leave me? What did I do so wrong to make him go; he promised we would be together forever. He said he loved me then he left me behind." Resignedly she said, "Maybe Cybil finally convinced him I wasn't good enough." Rubbing her hand over her still flat stomach, "He said he didn't want our babies, what am I going to do, how do you I tell my child his father didn't want them?"

Richard's heart nearly broke as he tried to reassure her, "Honey, I don't know what went wrong but I can guarantee it wasn't anything you did or didn't do. Blake was obviously having problems nobody knew because he didn't say anything."

"That's just it Rick, I should have known there was something wrong, if I hadn't been so selfish with wanting a baby so bad maybe he would still be here with me." Tears fell like rain from her sad eyes.

Richard wasn't going to let Mickie think this was all her fault. "Mickie you can't blame yourself, Blake's a grown man and makes his own decisions it was his choice to walk away. I'll have some of my people try and track him down and find out what is going on."

Mickie shook her head, "No Rick, if he wants out then I will have to accept his decision and raise our baby on my own."

George put his arm around his daughter, "Sweetie, both Rick and I will be there to help support and raise your baby and our grandchild you won't be on your own."

Richard agreed, "Absolutely and you can stay here for as long as you want."

Mickie shook her head, "I don't want to stay here without Blake; there are too many memories." She turned to her father, Daddy can I stay with until I get back on my feet?"

George hugged his daughter, "Of course Sweetheart, you can stay for as long as you like. It will be nice to have some company, be just like old times with the two of us and I'll be able to pamper you."

They could both see it was an effort for her to keep her eyes open, so they bundled her off to bed as the sedative worked its magic finally sending her into a dreamless sleep.

CHAPTER 7

UPON RE-ENTERING THE kitchen Richard was standing at the window he turned, with no gentle way to put it he stated; "Blake's back."

Even though she suspected that was the reason for the early morning visit her tummy still gave a flutter at the mention of his name.

"I know Dotty rang me last night just after he got in." Clutching her coffee cup she asked, "Do you know how long he will be here?"

Richard shook his head, "No, I didn't hang around to listen, Cybil being her usual self I'd have had a hard time getting a word in."

Mickie laughed, "Yes she does have a tendency to dominate a conversation especially if it has anything to do with Blake." Watching her father-in-law he looked worried, "What's really bothering you Rick?"

He reached across the table and gathered her hand in his, "I'm concerned for you. You have become such a strong, independent woman and I would hate for Blake's return to destroy all that and what of Dj, will you tell him his father's back? If you want I will make sure he never finds you or Dylan."

Mickie understood Rick's fear but she knew she would never return to the helpless lost soul she was when Blake left.

She was a well respected business woman, she had responsibilities and she wouldn't' turn her back on them like

Blake did, she was a better person than that. About telling Dylan of his father she would hold off on that, she wanted to know just what Blake's future plans were. She smiled reassuring Rick, "Don't worry that woman is long gone, I have Dj and responsibilities now, I won't hide from him but I won't actively court his attention either. If he finds me on his own then I'll deal with it but be assured I won't let him hurt me again, the first time nearly destroyed me. This time he will be playing by my rules and I have Dylan to think of, no one hurts my son not even his father."

Richards's fear abated slightly, his son would find a mature, strong independent woman; she was nothing like the young girl he left behind all those years ago.

Glancing at his watch he said, "I better leave so that you can get ready for work, how's the boutique going?"

Mickie's boutique sold the sexiest lingerie he had ever seen; he knew she wore her products and he sometimes wished he was thirty years younger.

A smile lit her face, "Would you believe I've had to triple the orders and Christmas is still four months away. I'm looking into expanding and starting an online shop, my research so far says it looks very promising. I am looking for the right programme to accommodate everything I need and to make it as simplistic as possible. I would only need two people to come in twice a week to fill and post orders, it would be a great job for someone that wanted to top up their pension." Cheekily she said, "So if you know of anyone send them my way."

Richard could hear the excitement in her voice he was pleased that all her hard work and efforts were making at least one of her dreams come true.

"I'd say you spent your inheritance very wisely, your Dad would be so proud of his little girl."

Tears misted her eyes, "I would never have made it if it weren't for the two of you, especially you Rick. You helped me through some very rough emotional times and I love you with all my heart. Without your support and guidance I wouldn't be the woman I am today and I thank you for being there."

Richard hugged her, "You have nothing to thank me for Sweetheart; you got to where you are from sheer determination, guts and hard work. You and Dylan mean more than anything to me; in fact you and Dj have been my saviours. When I thought I would go insane you gave me a refuge to be able to clear my head and get things into prospective."

Mickie remembered the months Richard stayed with them after her father's first heart attack, back then he seriously considered divorcing Cybil, her mood swings had become intolerable and her bouts of violence had sent Richard to the brink.

"You know there is always a place for you in our home for as long as you need."

Richard kissed her forehead, "You never know I might be taking you up on that offer sooner than later."

Mickie pulled back and looked into Richard's face, with concern she asked, "Are you alright, you're not sick are you?" She had lost her father too soon she didn't want to lose Richard too.

"No Honey, I'm as healthy as a horse. It's just that with Blake back I've decided to go through with the divorce."

This didn't surprise Mickie it had been on the cards for a long time. "Have you discussed it with her yet?" Knowing the wrath of thunder would reign down on him when he did.

Richard laughed harshly, "When does one have a discussion with Cybil especially when it's something as distasteful as discussing a divorce. I have approached her on several occasions but she starts ranting and raving about all the sacrifices she made and in the end I just walk away. Christ, we haven't slept together for over fifteen years and before that she only accepted me on sufferance 'Because it was her duty as a wife.' Mickie felt terrible for Richard, "Maybe I shouldn't have talked you out of it all those years ago, you could have found someone else by now and had some happiness."

"No," He assured her, "You were right, it wasn't the time. I can honestly say that I have no feelings for her at all, not love, not even hate, in fact all I feel for her is pity, she could have had so much but because of her bitterness and inability to give love she has nothing but her materialistic and superficial world. Those people she calls her 'friends' will drop her as soon as they hear of the divorce then all she will have is her empty palace."

Mickie's phone rang; she gave Richard a loving squeeze and went to answer it. Returning with a message, "That was your office they said Mr Holmes has rescheduled your meeting for this morning, if it's not convenient he will have to cancel until next week."

Richard had just finished wiping the cups, "No that's fine I better get going otherwise I'll make you late."

Mickie walked him to the door, "Are you still coming to dinner Sunday night?"

Richard had been coming to dinner every Sunday since Blake left it had become a kind of tradition, Dylan loved having his grandfather over and looked forward to it every week.

"Sure I haven't missed one yet." He smiled.

She smiled back, "No you haven't but with Blake back I thought you might want to spend some time with him?"

Richard laughed, "You're kidding right. That would be 'Mission Impossible' with Cybil around besides I'll have plenty of time to catch up with Blake." That settled he kissed her cheek, waved goodbye and headed to the office.

CHAPTER 8

MICKIE UNLOCKED THE door to "Unforgettable Moments," her lingerie boutique. She felt a sense of pride every time she entered knowing all the hard work she had done finally paid off, the continued success of her growing business not only proved to her but to others that she could make it in her own right.

She turned the 'Closed' sign over to 'Open' and headed to the rear of the shop where her office was located. After dealing with the morning mail, Mickie started checking off the latest inventory. The shop was busy most of the morning; a few regulars came in to see the new range plus a busload of tourists visiting the area called in to ooh and ahh over her vast array of lingerie. Mickie loved days like this they kept her busy and her mind off other things for a while.

Once again the bell over the door chimed, Mickie lifted her face with a ready smile to greet her new customer and was greeted herself with a megawatt one in return. The handsome man making his way to the counter had an arrogant swagger to his walk as though he dared anyone to stop him from reaching his destination.

"Hey Sweetheart, how's my favourite girl? He leant over the counter and placed a kiss on her cheek, "Can I talk you into having a late lunch with me?" his voice was husky liked he'd smoked too many cigarettes.

Mickie knew Kit Anderson would never pollute his body with such things; he was too much a health nut for that. Also he considered his body a temple and kept it in peak condition for all the women who seemed to be constantly throw themselves at him. Today he had tied his shoulder length blonde hair into a pony tail, on some men it would look ridiculous but on Kit it just enhanced his looks. He was an extremely handsome man with high cheek bones, a strong jaw line, straight nose and the greenest eyes she had ever seen. With the twinkle of mischief and his boyish charms she knew women found irresistible, they either wanted to cuddle him or bed him either way was fine with Kit, he was also her financial advisor.

Mickie laughed at his hopeful puppy dog look he had mastered to get his own way. "To answer your first question I'm fine, secondly I doubt very much I'm your favourite girl and thirdly I'm sorry but I have already eaten."

Kit gave her a wounded look, "How can you say that you're not my favourite girl, I'll have you know I don't say that every woman I know."

Mickie scoffed, "Sure Mr Anderson, the way I hear it that's your favourite line to get the ladies horizontal."

"Kit laughed admitting, "Yes well it has worked a time or two. You know I would give them all up if you accepted my proposal."

Mickie smiled, Kit had asked her to marry him on numerous occasions but she had never taken him seriously, she had too much baggage to work through before she even thought of a relationship. Looking at the man before her, if things were different she might very well have become Mrs Kit Anderson.

"Kit you would make some lady a wonderful husband but I'm not her and besides the girl that took you on would have to have the stamina of an all in wrestler to fight off all your other women."

He smiled smugly, "She'd need that kind of stamina for more than just fighting off the hordes." He wiggled his eyebrows.

"Well if I can't talk you into marrying me how about just taking me to bed?"

Mickie picked up the paper weight she had been playing with and threw it at Kit, "Mr Anderson you are truly outrageous and 'NO' I won't sleep with you!"

He caught it easily laughing, "Who said anything about sleeping? That would be the last thing on my mind if I had you naked and horizontal in bed."

Mickie blushed to the roots of her hair, she knew he was kidding around but talk like that always embarrassed her, changing the subject quickly she asked, "So what are you doing here other than harassing and embarrassing me?"

He knew he had embarrassed Mickie but sometimes she needed shaking up, she was far too young to shut herself off from love. She was beautiful, intelligent and so damn sexy; her ex-husband must have had rocks in his head to let her go. He had fallen in lust with Mickie the first time he had met her but gradually over the years it had turned into something much deeper. He swore to himself he would wait until she was ready to join the real world and when she was he want to be the man she turned to.

"Well, I've actually come to ask a favour, would you accompany me to a charity dinner tonight?"

Mickie was about to refuse when she reconsidered, Dylan was at Kathie's for the weekend and all she would be doing is watching a movie on TV so she accepted much to Kit's delight.

He was pleasantly surprised, he thought she would have declined as she had done every other time he'd asked, "Great I will pick you up at your place around seven is that ok?"

"Sure I will close the shop half an hour early give me plenty of time to get ready."

He kissed her on the cheek, before leaving the store he turned and said, "Wear something sexy I want to be the envy of every male there and no backing out." With a wave of his hand he closed the door behind him.

CHAPTER 9

B LAKE SPENT MOST of the day visiting some of their old haunts, all of them bringing back one memory after another of the times him and Mickie had spent there; God he missed her so much. He had been such a fool leaving her like that. There wasn't a day go by that something or another, a smell, a laugh wouldn't trigger a thought of her. A couple of times he had tried to rid himself of her memory in the arms of other women especially after he received the divorce papers but it was always her face her saw, her body he was touching and her name he called out.

It was the reason he stopped dating, he knew Mickie was the only woman for him.

He went to the home they had shared and asked the new owners if they had a forwarding address for Mickie, they told him the house had been empty up until a year ago when they bought it. Now Blake was really confused his Mother told him Mickie had sold the house and moved away not long after he left. He made further enquiries with his old neighbours and wasn't happy with what he had learned, he and his Mother were going to have a little discussion when he got home, she had some explaining to do. He had caught up with a few of their friends even thought their greeting was cordial it wasn't the same as before he left, their manner got considerably colder when he asked questions about Mickie.

Blake had a feeling their friends knew a lot more but weren't going to tell him. He went to the Sullivan family home only to find that it had been resold and the current occupants had no forwarding address for the previous owners. It was like they had disappeared off the face of the earth. Someone somewhere knew where his wife was, she wouldn't just up and leave like that, sever all contact with her friends that just wasn't Mickie. Checking his watch he saw it was late, getting in his car he headed home.

Richard and Cybil were already in the formal lounge when Blake walked in. His father stood by the fire with a whiskey in his hand, his mother sat rigid on the sofa her face contorted in anger. The hostile atmosphere was thick enough to cut with a knife; it was obvious he had come in at the end of an unpleasant conversation by the look of his Mother. They both acknowledged him as the door bell rang; Blake watched as his Mother's face turn from sheer hatred to social hostess in the blink of an eye, she rose to greet her guests.

Blake joined his Father by the fire as his Mother's guests entered the room; he groaned inwardly as Olivia James entered, he now understood his Mother's urgency to be home for dinner. She smiled at him as she made her way to his side.

Olivia had been after Blake for years, not just for the prestige of being associated with The Hunter family, one of the richest in the country but because he was so damn gorgeous. When he started dating Mickie Sullivan everyone thought it was to vex his Mother, Olivia had tried every one of her feminine wiles to lure Blake away but to no avail, to everyone's surprise he genuinely love Mickie and married her. Olivia had always been jealous of Mickie throughout their school years, granted she was pretty and had a good figure, if not a bit too voluptuous for someone so small, but she too also had a good body. Mickie always had people flocking around her mostly boys, like bees to honey, if she showed the slightest interest in one of the boys Olivia would sleep with them just to prove she could have any boy Mickie wanted. That was until Blake; it still ate at her that he had chosen a no body, someone without any breeding or money over her.

Cybil had told Olivia of Blake's return home and she already knew of his divorce, now was her chance to snatch up one of the richest men in the country and no matter what, she would have Blake Hunter.

Richard stood watching Cybil's friends, he hated these parties the people were all so fake. By the look on his son's face he felt the same way, one of Cybil's protégés was crawling all over him, he was having a hard time keeping the woman's hands off him. He watched his wife turn from a spitting viper into the gracious society hostess attending to her guests needs.

Earlier he had decided to inform her he would be starting divorce proceedings, he wanted some happiness before he died. She predictably lost her temper threatened to take him for everything, not that this bothered him he had made sure she was well looked after. She swore she would drag it on for years to which Richard laughed, explaining that as they hadn't lived as man and wife for over fifteen years there wouldn't be any waiting period only the formality of submitting the paperwork and waiting for the judge's decree. Richard was giving her the house plus a generous allowance for the rest of her life, the rest would be sorted out by their respective lawyers, all he wanted was his freedom.

Blake caught his Father's eye giving him a quizzical look, Richard shrugged his shoulders and went and got another drink.

Olivia smiled up at Blake and purred, "Hello Handsome, fancy you seeing you back to town." Fishing for information, she enquired, "You going to be here long?"

Blake looked down at Olivia even though she was a pretty woman she did nothing for him, she had the morals of an alley cat, been married three times, each husband richer than the last, he knew his Mother had orchestrated this meeting she had been throwing Olivia at him for years but he wasn't interested and if she or his Mother thought there will be anything happening between them they would both be sadly disappointed.

Detaching her hand from his arm he said, "Depends, I have some things I need to sort out after that I'm not sure."

"Are they business things?" she felt he was being evasive.

"No personal. Why so interested in what I'm up to?" he'd do some fishing of his own.

"Just wondering? Your Mother said you and Mickie had divorced. I know what that's like, I'm on my third. I don't know why I seem to marry the wrong men; statistically they say girls usually marry men from their home towns, maybe that's where I've gone wrong."

"I wouldn't know about that."

"That's right you married a hometown girl and it ended in divorce but then she wasn't from the same calibre."

Blake anger was growing with every word coming out of Olivia's mouth; he knew of her jealousy of his wife, Mickie was ten times the better person. She wasn't shallow or always looking for the next free buck she could get, as long as she had a roof over her head, food in the cupboard and clothes on her back she was happy unlike the harpy beside him.

He was just about to give her a mouthful when the dinner gong went; he swallowed the remainder of his drink in one mouthful looking for someone to rescue him unfortunately everyone had gone. Walking past his Mother he noticed she gave Olivia a wink which angered him even more, he and his Mother would be having an in depth discussion in the morning, he would not tolerate her interference in his life again.

CHAPTER 10

ON THE OTHER side of town Kit pulled into Mickie's driveway, he couldn't believe she had accepted his dinner invitation and not backed out at the last minute. Mickie usually stayed away from these events in case she ran into Cybil and her cronies, he knew there was bad blood between them but didn't know what.

Mickie was in her room putting the finishing touches to her outfit. She saw Kit's headlights in the driveway; she took a last look at herself in the full length mirror. She had piled her long dark hair on top of her head with several curled strands hanging down at the side, securing it with diamante clips. She loved the way her long midnight blue halter dress hugged her curves. Her bust, which she considered too big for the rest of her body, filled the top admirably, the skirt split daringly to her thigh showing off a considerable length of shapely leg. She had placed a rhinestone choker around her neck, a diamante bracelet on her wrist, and diamond drop earrings in her ears and last but not least a dab of channel No5 between her breasts, on her wrists and behind her ears, she slipped on her silver hi-heels just as Kit rang the bell. Grabbing her bag and shawl off the bed she went to answer the door.

Kit turned as he heard the door open, for a moment he stood there speechless the vision before him was breathtaking, he considered Mickie a beautiful woman but this person standing in front of him was absolutely stunning.

"Wow," he finally got out when his vocal cords decided to work. "You took me at my word when I said to wear something sexy."

Mickie looked down at herself and started to have reservations, maybe it was too much. "Um if you hang on a minute I go and put something else on."

Kit reached for her arm, "Don't you dare I'm going to be the envy of every man there including the married ones. Mind you I'll be fighting off the hyenas all night." He was worried if she went back inside she wouldn't come out, giving her his best smile he pulled her towards him shutting the front door.

"Sweetheart you look beautiful." He helped her into the car.

It was a fifteen minute drive to get to the venue, there was valet parking so Kit drove up to the front door, after relinquishing his keys to the porter Kit went around and opened Mickie's door. As she stepped out he groaned, her dress split near up to her hip revealing the most beautiful leg he had seen, it was going to be a very long night. He was right about her being the centre of attention, heads of both men and women were turning to see who the glamorous woman on his arm was. They speculated she was a model or movie star, as they made their way through the foyer they were stopped by a myriad of people all wanting to be introduced to her, many were shocked when they found out who she was.

Rob Mansfield, one of his partners caught his eye the moment he stepped into the banquet room, motioning with his head that he wanted to speak to him; Kit excused himself leaving Mickie to talk to one of her customers.

Kit grabbed a glass of champagne from a passing waiter as Rob asked, "Who is the Babe and does she have a sister?"

The lascivious look Rob was giving Mickie was pissing Kit off, usually it didn't bother him if Rob lusted after his dates but this was different, this was Mickie.

"Wipe your chin Rob and put your tongue back in your head, she's a client and off limits." There was a strict rule in the company, 'There would be no dating clients'. Companies could lose business real quick if Management started sleeping with their clientele.

Rob looked at Kit in amazement, "I've never seen that woman before in my life and be assured if she was on the books I would have made it my number one priority to know who she was."

Kit laughed, "Man you have met her a hundred times but I admit never looking like this."

Now Rob was really confused, surely he would have remembered meeting her, she was a goddess and he wanted her in his bed.

She was making her way to the two men he whispered, "Quick tell me who she is." Kit kept quiet.

A Mickie walked towards the two men, the eyes of every man followed her across the room, as she reached Kit's side she slipped her arm through his as she greeted Rob.

"Hello Rob, how Alice or is Alicia I can never keep up with your women you change them so often."

Rob was flabbergasted, "Mickie Sullivan is that you? Good God woman, where have you been hiding that gorgeous body of yours? If I knew you looked like this I would never have given my old mate here your account."

Mickie blushed to the roots of her hair; Rob was all but drooling, his eyes bulging out of his head. Kit was getting really annoyed with Rob now, firstly for embarrassing Mickie and secondly for the way he was ogling Mickie's chest, it was like he'd never seen a pair of breasts before, Kit decided, was time to circulate.

"You'll have to excuse us Rob, I've just seen the Mayor and I want a word." With saying that, he ushered Mickie away.

Kyle apologized for Rob's behaviour, "Sorry about that, Rob turns into a horse's ass when he's had a few."

Mickie thanked him for the rescue, "Is he always like that?"

He nodded, "Pretty much, he gets worse the more he drinks so I think we will keep our distance from him for the rest of the night."

Mickie agreed, "That's fine by me."

The rest of the evening went well. The dinner raised over two hundred and fifty thousand dollars for the local children's hospital enabling them to upgrade some of their outdated equipment.

Most of the night Kit had his hand full keeping lecherous, drunk men away from Mickie, he regretted telling her to dress sexy, not for her sake but for his. She was living breathing sex on legs, every guy's wet dream come true. He couldn't blame his brothers-in-arms wanting to take her home but she came with him she was leaving with him. Rob tried several time throughout the evening to dance with her and Kit would cut in every time, the more Rob drank the cruder he got.

At one stage Mickie laughed up at Kit, "Are you going to chase them all off, all they are doing is dancing."

He shook his head, "No Sweetheart that's not what they are doing. They are rubbing themselves against you, imagining they are making love to you."

"Really, are you serious?" she was amazed.

"Absolutely" He knew this because it was what he was doing with her in his arms.

"Even the octogenarian?"

Smiling he replied, "Especially him, he wishes he was fifty years younger, you could give the old boy a heart attack."

With that they both burst out laughing, turning the heads of the other dancers to see what was so amusing. They made a striking couple, Kit being tall, blonde and lean and Mickie's slight build and exotic looks.

After saying their goodbyes they headed for Mickie's home, it was well after midnight and with Dj away she was going to enjoy a well deserved sleep in.

They pulled into the driveway; Mickie turned to Kyle and invited him in for coffee, he declined.

"Sweetheart if I come in it won't be for coffee and I don't think you're ready for that."

Mickie blushed, "No you're right Kit. I have some things I need to sort out before I think of starting a relationship but if and when I'm ready you will be the first to know."

Kit was the first man since Blake that she felt a spark of interest in. She had never thought herself as a sensual or sexual woman; she hadn't been with a man in over six years, not since Blake left. Lately she had been seriously thinking that she should start dating, she wanted to feel like a woman again and not just Dylan's Mum; she wouldn't do a one night stand and she knew she wasn't ready for anything more serious especially now that Blake was back. But she would do something soon.

"God Mickie, you shouldn't say things like that to a guy who's be celibate for the last six months, he might try and change your mind." Kit could feel the front of his pants tightening, if he wasn't careful he would embarrass himself.

Mickie knew Kit wouldn't force himself on her but she did wonder what it would be like to have him kiss her.

If Mickie didn't stop looking at his mouth, licking her lips, he was going to have to show her exactly what his lips could do.

"Sweetheart if you don't get out of the car in the next three seconds I'm going to kiss you."

Her tongue came out, glistened her lips; that was all the invitation he needed. He crossed the space between them slowly enough that she had time to pull away, the moment their lips met he was a goner. She tasted of strawberries and champagne, a heady combination, his tongue traced the line of her closed lips she parted them, letting him in. He became instantly hard groaning into her mouth.

Mickie felt a tingle spread though her body from her head to her toes as Kyle's mouth closed on hers. She was overwhelmed with sensations; it had been such a long time since someone had kissed her with passion. Her nipples hardened and her breast swelled waiting to be caressed. She could taste the whiskey on his tongue and something else… man. She had miss being this intimate with a man, her hand went to his cheek and she ran it through his hair which was surprisingly soft.

Kit reluctantly pulled away from her lips, holding her at arm's length breathing hard, "Honey if we keep going, you are going to be naked and beneath me in your bed in the next five minutes and I don't think you want that just yet, so I will be a gentleman and walk you to the front door then go home and have an extremely long cold shower."

Mickie's body didn't want Kit to stop but her head said she wasn't ready to go to bed with him either, so she nodded at his request.

As he got out of the car he pulled the front of his shirt out over his pants to cover his erection, he was harder than granite.

He helped Mickie out of the car and walked her to the front door taking her keys unlocking the door.

Stepping over the threshold she turned to him, "Thankyou for a wonderful evening Kit, I'm sorry it didn't turn out better for you."

Kit caressed her face, "Sweetheart it was everything I wanted. I got to spend an enjoyable evening with a beautiful, desirable woman; I was the envy of every man at the dinner and if I haven't scared her off she may want to do it again. No off you go before I forget I'm a gentleman and ravish you on your doorstep"

Without saying a word she leant forward kissed him on the lips turned and closed the door.

Kit stood there for several minutes before returning to the car, it was definitely going to be a long night and no matter how many cold showers he took he wouldn't be getting to sleep anytime soon.

CHAPTER 11

THE WEEKEND PASSED pleasantly for Mickie, she picked Dj up from Kathie's just after lunch and they spent the afternoon at the park. She loved these times with Dylan; he was a ball of energy and constantly on the go. This was when she got to see the world through the innocence of a child's eye, where everything was an adventure and the ugly side of life hadn't touched. It was times like this she thought of Blake and what he was missing, the joy and wonder on Dj's face as a duck came up and took a piece of bread from his hand. When he pretended to be a starship captain flying high above the sky on the swing or a daredevil ridding the white water rapids as he slid down the slide. She was saddened at the loss for both Blake and Dylan, even though Richard filled the male role admirably, the loving relationship between a father and son would never be and the years that had passed could never be recaptured. The sun was slowly setting so it was time to head home, Mickie called out to Dj, Richard would be at the house soon and she needed to finish cooking their dinner, it was a lovely ending to the weekend.

At yet another dinner party at the Hunter home to which Richard was rapidly getting sick of attending, he was summoned to his office to answer the phone, Blake entered not long after to see his father pulling on his coat and grabbing his car keys.

"Dad is everything okay?"

"I have something I have to attend to urgently, could you make my apologies to your Mother and her guests?"

"Sure, is there anything I can do?"

Richard shook his head, "No it will be fine and I'll explain it all to you when I get back."

Mickie's call had Richard breaking speed limits as he made his way to her home. It seems someone had broken into her shop and the police had asked if she would attend.

Mickie was waiting at the front door when he pulled up, as he came up the path he asked, "What's the damage?"

Mickie shrugged her shoulders, "Not sure exactly. The police said the front door had been kicked in and a lot of the stock had been thrown around the room. They said my office had received the most damage and just wanted me to go down and see if anything has been taken. Dylan's in bed but not asleep, I've told him I have to go to the store and that you would be coming over to look after him. He is thrilled; he has been stock piling all the stories you are going to read"

Richard laughed, "That's ok he's usually asleep before I get through the first one, you get going and call me and let me know if you need me to come down."

She kissed his cheek, "Thanks Rick for coming, I know you had guests for dinner and I've probably put you in hot water with Cybil."

He shrugged, "So what else is new, don't worry I can handle Cybil, you get going."

Mickie's mind was in turmoil as she pulled up outside the shop. Police cars were everywhere, officers were interviewing pedestrians others taking photos. As she locked her door an officer excused himself from a group of men in blue overalls and walked towards her.

"Ma'am, are you Ms Sullivan?" He enquired.

"Yes."

"Ma'am I'm officer Adam Peters, before you go into the store I would like to ask you a few questions?"

"Okay."

Ma'am, can you think of anyone that would have a grudge against you, Want to cause you any harm?"

Mickie shook her head, "No, well maybe my ex mother-in-law but this sort of thing would be beneath even her."

"And she would be?" he enquired.

"Cybil Hunter.

The officer raised his eyebrow, everyone knew who Cybil Hunter was but he didn't know she had a daughter-in-law. He nodded in agreement, "No I wouldn't think she would have had a hand in this. Can you think of anyone else, a disgruntled customer or maybe an ex-employee?"

Mickie chewed on her bottom lip, "No, there isn't anyone I can think of at the moment."

Officer Peters studied the woman in front of him. She would have been all of five foot five inches in height, slender built but rounded in all the right places. Her long dark hair was pulled back into ponytail; she had a heart shaped face with the biggest blue eyes he had ever seen, she was a strikingly beautiful woman. He knew she was scared but he needed to prepare her for what she would find when she entered the premises. "Ma'am I need to inform you that there is considerable damage most of it is centred in your office. There is a lot of stock thrown around the shop; we surmise that was done as they were leaving. It was a good thing you had an alarm system they were only in there for a short period of time before we turned up."

Mickie felt a sense of dread creep over her, even though she hadn't seen the extent of the damage from what the officer told her she guessed it was going to be awful.

The officer placed a guiding hand on her arm and led her into the store.

The showroom looked like a bomb had gone off; most of the stock was on the floor, displays upended, shelving broken even though this looked bad she knew the officer wasn't referring to it when he warned her.

She stopped short of entering her office and took a deep calming breath; the officer beside her understood her trepidation but encouraged her to go on.

The sight before her was devastating; files had been strewn all over the room, her plants had been ripped out of their pots and her desk had been cut in two but it was the message on the wall that stopped her from breathing.

The words were written in red paint most likely to assimilate blood and read, "YA GUNNA BE NEXT BITCH. YOU WILL PAY FOR WHAT YOU DID TO ME. NO ONE SELLS ME OUT AND GETS AWAY WITH IT WHEN I FIND YOU YOURE DEAD!!!!!!!"

For the life of her, Mickie couldn't think of anyone who could hate her that much to do this, not even Cybil's hatred would go this far.

CHAPTER 12

MICKIE SPENT A good portion of the night with the police trying to answer their questions. While she was standing amongst the wreckage in the front of the shop, someone tapped her on the shoulder.

"Excuse me Ma'am are you Ms Sullivan?" Mickie turn to see a gentleman in overalls, "Yes can I help you?"

"Ma'am, I'm John Edwards. Mr. Hunter went me over to fix a broken door."

Mickie hadn't even thought about getting the door repaired she was glad Richard had.

"Um you will probably have to ask one of the officers over there," she pointed to a group of men standing off to the side. "I'm sorry everything's a bit of a mess."

Looking around John thought that was an understatement, someone had certainly trashed the place.

The next morning Dylan was up with the birds but hadn't beaten his Grandfather, Richard was on the phone when Dj wondered into the kitchen, finishing the call he greeted his grandson.

"Hey, how's my boy this fine morning?"

Dylan loved having his grandfather stay over, he read him three books last night; he always made him his favourite breakfast.

"Good, Grampa can I have some crambled eggs please?" Dylan climbed up onto the stool under the breakfast bar reaching for the glass of milk his grandfather had placed there.

"Certainly Sir and would like some bacon with that order?" Dylan laughed at his grandfather impersonation of a butler, "Yup and lots of cheese please." Richard got busy preparing Dj's breakfast, hearing the shower turn off and grabbed a cup down to pour Mickie a coffee.

Moments later she entered the kitchen ruffling Dylan's hair, accepting the cup Richard held out for her.

"So how are my two favourite men?"

Dylan laughed, "I not a man Mummy I a little boy"

Mickie smiled down at her son ruffling his hair, "So you are."

Looking over at Richard who was dishing up Dylan's breakfast,

"I see you conned Grandpa into cooking you breakfast this morning.

"Yep and he is making it with lots of cheese, do you want some Mummy, you can share mine."

"Thank you darling but I will settle for coffee just now."

While Dylan ate his breakfast Mickie gave Richard an update on the previous night.

"Rick, for the life of me I cannot think of anyone that would hate me that much, except for Cybil. I know in my heart she wouldn't have anything to do with this, especially to write such a horrific massage. The violence in the attack on my office was pure hatred, whoever it was put an axe through my desk and tore my plant to shreds."

"Sweetheart I've hire a security company to keep an eye on the place and I've got Mike sending out people to see if they can pick up some information on the street. It doesn't look like its street crime this sounds more personal to me. Are you going in this morning?"

"Yes the police would have finished all their forensic stuff now I just have to clean up."

"If you don't mind I would like to come with you and get Mike to meet us there?" Mike was Richard's head of security at Hunter Engineering.

"Okay, that would be great I was actually going to ask Kit to meet me there as I really didn't want to go there on my own."

Mickie walked over and gave Richard a kiss on the cheek.

Puzzled he asked, "What was that for?"

"That was thank you for last night. Coming over to look after Dj and for sending the repair man to fix my door, I was in such a state that it didn't even occur to me how I would secure the shop."

"You're welcome and you did me a favour getting me out of another dreary dinner party." He laughed.

"Oh my god, that's right. Cybil is going to have your head for that. Oh well that's just another thing for her to lie at my door."

"Honey, don't worry about it. With Blake home all her energies are concentrating on him she probably didn't even noticed I had gone."

Mickie raised and eyebrow, Cybil noticed everything especially if her husband ducked out in the middle of one of her shindigs without a word.

He laughed at her sceptical look, "Okay she probably did notice but hey, she'll rant and rave for five minutes, I'll walk out and she will go on with something else." Checking his watch, he grabbed his jacket.

"I'll better get going and face the music, I will meet you at the shop in an hour." Richard kissed to the top of Dylan's head as he headed out the door.

Mickie finished the dishes and got Dylan ready for school.

CHAPTER 13

AT THE HUNTER home Cybil was sitting across from Blake at the breakfast table looking like a volcano about to erupt. He noticed his father hadn't returned from his trip last night. Earlier Blake had informed his Mother that he had been to the house and the information he'd discovered. She had been slamming things down on the table ever since; Blake knew she wouldn't be able to hold her temper in for much longer.

Cybil's fury was mounting by the minute, not only had Richard embarrassed her in front of her friends by leaving without a word in the middle of her dinner and still hadn't returned but Blake had blatantly disobeyed her and had gone looking for that trollop he married.

The quiet was soon shattered when Cybil could no long contain herself and Blake copped both barrels.

Her voice reverberated around the room, "What do you mean you went to the house, I had already informed you that tramp you married sold it years ago. Why are you digging around old ground? You left her behind in the first place remember, so why are you looking for her now you should have known she only married you for your money?" Blake shook his head; his Mother never understood anything about Mickie, money that was the one thing she was never interested in.

"Why thank you Mother for thinking all I have going for me is my bank balance."

Cybil started to deny this when Blake held up his hand to stop her before she started.

"Strange that the new owners only bought the house a year ago up until then the rates and electricity were still being paid, you wouldn't happen to know who was doing that would you Mother?"

Cybil knew there was no use in denying the accusation Blake obviously knew who had been making the payments. Waving it off she said, "So what If I kept the house going I did buy it for you as a wedding present, I just kept it going in case you came back."

"Then why lie and tell me Mickie had sold it. Where did the money go from the sale?"

"It went into your trust fund of course; I wasn't letting that bitch get her hands on any of your money." She was so fired up she couldn't even say Mickie's name.

"Your jealousy of Mickie is bordering on insanity Mother. She has done nothing to warrant it. Mickie was always polite and respectful towards you and your friends even when she had every right to tell you all to go to hell. Time and time again she tried to resolve the situation between the both of you not just for your sake or hers but for mine and every time she did you slapped her down. I want you to listen very carefully to what I have to say. I love Mickie with my heart I never stopped, I intend to find her and when I do and if she will forgive me I am going to ask her to marry me and there is nothing you can say or do to change that."

Cybil couldn't' believe what she was hearing, after everything she had done to finally getting that woman out of her son's life this is how he was going to repay her, she couldn't control herself and exploded, "Over my dead body!

That woman will never be welcomed into this family as long as I take breath and I absolutely forbid you to pursue this ridiculous notion. You will marry someone with the right breeding, one with a proper standing in the community and one that comes with a substantial dowry."

Blake interrupted her, "If you're thinking of putting Olivia James in the picture for that you can forget it, she has the morals of an alley cat, has slept with half the male population of this town, so be assured that will never happen."

Cybil ignored Blake and continued, "A woman that will give you children that others look up to, what you won't do is hook up with some harlot from the wrong side of town, I will not let another bitch from that family take what is mine, do you hear me not after all I have done to keep her out of this family." Cybil was pacing the room like a caged tiger.

Blake's jaw dropped, his mind was going ten to the dozen, what the hell was his Mother talking about and what had she done. "So Mother what exactly did you do to keep Mickie out of the family?"

Before Blake got his answer his Father entered the room to see what all the shouting was about, he could hear it as soon as he opened the front door. His Mother turned on him with the speed of a cobra, spitting venom.

"Spent the night with your whore again did you?" She spat on the floor, "You disgust me. How dare you leave the middle of one of my parties, without so much as a word to go be with her and embarrass me in front of my friends."

Blake's gasp spurred her on, "That's right Blake your father prefers the company of prostitutes, I guess that's the only way people like him can get sex, by paying for it."

Her accusations didn't faze Richard he had heard them all so many times before but he didn't want Blake to thinks they were true.

"Sorry Cybil but the only time I have ever had to 'pay for sex' as you so eloquently put it is with you."

Cybil went berserk, "How dare you say I'm no better than a whore, you've given me nothing."

"Really, so what are all those designer clothes, furs and jewellery in your cupboard if not for services rendered? Mind you I think you owe me seeing I haven't been in your bed for over fifteen years, then again I wouldn't want to risk getting frost bite from an ice queen like you."

It was the first time in Blake's life he'd ever heard his Father speak to his mother in such a way and it was the first time he saw his Mother lost for words.

Cybil couldn't believe what was happening, both men in her family falling for the same trollop, she knew Richard spent time with Blake's whore and bastard son but if she told him he would then find out how to get in touch with her and she prefer to lose her husband than her son to that woman. Cybil could feel the room closing in on her, both men watched as she start gasping for breath next thing they knew she was on the floor having some kind of fit. Both raced to her, Cybil's eyes were rolled back in her head, her body thrashing around, if Richard didn't know better he would have thought she was having an epileptic seizure.

Blake grabbed the phone and called for an ambulance, after several minutes she stopped moving and just lay there so still. Richard called out to her but there was no response. He checked her pulse and found it racing, if they didn't lower it somehow she would either have a heart attack or stroke.

The ambulance arrived in record time; Dotty showed them into the room, Doc Addams the family physician followed close behind the gurney. Richard was surprised to see him, he explained his presence.

"I was heading back from transporting a patient to the Hospice when the call came in." Richard nodded and let Pete Addams access to his wife. He examined Cybil quickly to assess if there was any immediate danger, once satisfied there wasn't he allowed her to be loaded onto the stretcher and taken to the hospital for a more thorough examination.

Blake followed his Father into his study, "Geez Dad what the hell just happened?"

"I think your Mother's had a complete breakdown. I've been expecting it for a while, actually ever since you left. Her mood swings and violent out bursts have been increasing, I had to ask Dotty back as your Mother assaulted every person I employed male or female, no one would work here, you do realise she has a problem?"

Blake nodded, "Yes. Before you came in I told her I had been looking for Mickie and that when I find her I was going to ask her to marry me, she went ballistic. I don't understand Mother's hatred of her."

Richard tried to explain, "Your Mother was jealous of Mickie's Mother, Lisbeth. Same as Mickie, people seem to flock to her, she was always laughing, always had a smile on her face. Lisbeth was the first to help anyone in need, the only thing she didn't have was standing or money unlike your Mother. Cybil couldn't understand why she was so popular and even though your Mother was pretty, Lisbeth was stunningly beautiful, Mickie looks very much like her. People were stunned when she chose to marry George Sullivan; she could have had any one of the titled chaps in the area but she picked a hard working plain looking ordinary guy with no money. George was a friend of your Mothers before Lisbeth moved to town, I think Cybil had a crush on George but because he had no money her parents would never have agreed for her to date him. George fell head over heels for Lisbeth, the love they had for each other was clearly there for everyone to see and when Mickie arrived they considered themselves truly blessed. Doctors had told Lisbeth she couldn't have any children due to a childhood illness. You were two then and because everyone made such a fuss over Lisbeth and her beautiful baby girl, your Mother decided she wanted another child, more importantly it had to be a girl. Unfortunately Cybil had a fall early on in the pregnancy and lost the baby, sustaining injuries that meant she wouldn't be able to have any more children. She was devastated, we looked to surrogacy was even about to finalize everything and your Mother pulled out said it wouldn't be the same if it didn't come from her. It was then she turned her anger, hurt and loss onto Lisbeth, everyone would gush how pretty Mickie was, what a good baby she was and as she grew from child to teenager then into an adult your Mother saw once again a Sullivan was taking the limelight even though neither woman pursued it. When Lisbeth was struck down with cancer and died your Mother was overjoyed but then when everyone sympathised with Mickie losing her mother so young Cybil turned that hatred onto Mickie. Then you came along and had the miss fortune to fall in love with the enemy. Cybil could see that once again a Sullivan was moving in on her territory and targeting the one thing Cybil loved above all else, You. So instead of forming a relationship with Mickie, she tried everything she could to push her away I guess she thought if you had to choose between the two of them you would pick your Mother. When you told Cybil you two would be married, I thought your Mother would have Mickie killed, by then she knew who you would pick if push came to shove and I think that was the final straw and it was another sin to lie at Mickie's door."

"Dad before you arrived, Mother said she had done things to keep Mickie out of the family, do you have any idea what she was talking about?"

Richard shook his head, "No Son sorry but your Mother and I hardly ever spoke or spent any time together. The only time I saw her happy since you've been gone was when she found out you had partitioned Mickie for a divorce.

Blake wasn't going to get the blame for that, "Dad it wasn't me who partitioned for the divorce. I was devastated when the papers arrived I never had any intentions of divorcing Mickie in actual fact it was around then that I had decided to move back but when the papers arrived I didn't bother. I thought I had put her through enough and if she wanted to end our marriage I didn't have the right to stop her."

Richard was stunned, "Blake Mickie never partitioned for the divorce, I was with her when she was served the papers it nearly destroyed her coming so soon after losing her Dad. She always thought you would come back for her she said you just needed time.

Blake was glad he was sitting down or he would have fallen, quietly he asked, "When and how did George die and why didn't anyone tell me?"

Richard watched the tears stream down his Son's cheeks, the shock of finding out his father-in-law had passed away was devastating.

"He died two years after you left. He had a series of heart attacks; the last one he didn't survive, seems he had a faulty valve. Cybil said she had spoken to you and that you wouldn't be able to make the funeral due to work commitments. That's when Mickie realised you wouldn't be coming back, she knew how close you were to George and for you not to turn up to his funeral, she said you must have really hated her."

Blake sat with his head in his hands his tears falling to the carpet, his grief turning to anger at his Mother. Standing up he started pacing the floor, "God Mother has a lot to answer for, I gather this is what she meant about keeping Mickie out of the family. Dad believe me if I had known about George being ill nothing would have stopped me being there and Mickie couldn't be further from the truth I could never hate her, she's my other half, I need her as much as I need air to breathe."

"I guess your Mother didn't want to take the chance that if you came back here you and Mickie might hook up again.

Blake was adamant, "There would be no doubt about that and I would have taken Mickie back with me."

Richard asked, "Why did you leave?"

Blake sighed, "There were several contributing factors, Mother's increscent pressure to join the firm and her constantly orchestrating dinners and lunches with her friend's daughters. Steve had presold a dozen copies of the programme I was working on, only it had major problems that I couldn't figure out how to fix. Even though Mickie never said I could see the disappointment in her face with every month that went by and she wasn't pregnant. To tell you the truth the thought of becoming a father back then terrified me. It was one thing after another and I just couldn't cope, so I took the coward's way out and left thinking that would solve everything, when in fact it only made it worse. It didn't take me long to realize I left the best thing that ever happened to me behind. I tried to call her but there was no answer, so I asked Mother to get Mickie to contact me, that's when she told me Mickie had sold the house and moved out of the area."

"Why didn't you come back then and find her yourself?" Blake shrugged his shoulders, "I was feeling pretty sorry for myself by then and figured I didn't deserve the right to force her into going with me?"

"So why wait so long before you decided to get a divorce?"

Blake was confused, "Dad I didn't instigate the divorce. I was gutted when the papers arrived, I sat on them for months and I tried every avenue to find her, even threatening her solicitor if he didn't set up a meeting with her. He told me she didn't want to see me ever again so I signed the damn papers and then went out got myself hammered."

Richard could see Cybil's handy work here, "Well Son, Mickie hurt the same, she said if you wanted a divorce that bad you could come and tell her to her face that you didn't love her, then and only then was she going to sign. Your solicitor rang her constantly demanding she sign the documents, after a couple of months I guess he just wore her down and she signed them. She always believed you would come back to her. I must admit you were very generous in your settlement even if she did burn your cheque."

Blake couldn't believe it, "Dad I never wrote out a cheque, my papers said she was happy with the money she got from the sale of the house and furnishings. Are you saying Mickie had nothing to do with the divorce?" He was really pissed now.

Richard shook his head, "No. She always said you would come back to her once you sorted yourself out, it was taking longer than she thought it would but she loved you with all her heart." Blake remembered around that time his Mother was on the phone to him almost daily, he turned to his father, "Do you think Mother instigated this whole thing?"

"I wouldn't count her out not being involved, but to get it through the courts not even she has that much power. Did you get your final decree?"

Blake shook his head, "Come to think of it, I don't remember."

"Well if I were you I would be checking to see if it was actually lodged, you both could still be married. How long before you go back?"

"I'm not, Steve bought me out and now I do consultancy work for him and the Government. I taking time off, I want to find Mickie and explain everything to her and hopefully she will forgive me and give me a second chance. I want to get married again and start that family she always wanted I just hope she hasn't found anyone else. Firstly though I need to check some things out so when I see her I have what I need to show her I didn't want a divorce."

The phone in Richard's office ring, it was Doc Addams from the hospital. Cybil's diagnosis wasn't good, he planned to keep her in for a couple of days or so to see if there was any change, at this time it looked like she had a total neurological breakdown, she was breathing on her own but that was about it.

The door bell rang, moments later Olivia James rushed into Richard's office, "Oh my god I just heard about Cybil, is she going to be all right?"

Richard spoke to Peter whilst Blake dealt with Olivia.

Blake groaned Olivia was the last person he wanted to see, his upbringing wouldn't let him be rude and tell her to buggar off. "She is resting comfortably at the hospital; Doc Addams is running a series of tests we won't know anything more for a couple of days."

Olivia saw this as an omen, her chance to make a move on Blake. With his Mother in hospital they would need someone to run the household until she was fit enough to do it herself. Olivia would offer her services, she had been grooming herself for this her whole life and with any luck she would be in Blake's bed by the end of the week.

"Well I'll go home pack a bag and come back," She was ticking things off in her mind. "You will need someone to run the house and organise things for you while Cybil is recuperating."

Both men were quick to reject that idea, "That won't be necessary Olivia," Richard said getting in first. "Thankyou for your kind offer but Dotty is here, she will make sure everything runs smoothly."

"But what about your dinner parties, she really isn't suitable to host them," she objected.

"There won't be any, at least not in the near future; that would be in bad taste don't you think, especially while Cybil is so ill."

She was getting desperate; she could see her chance slipping away. "What about her charities someone will need to see to them." Richard thought for a moment, someone would need to oversee things until Cybil got back on her feet; it would also keep Olivia out of their hair.

"Well if you could find time in your busy schedule; that would be very helpful." Olivia breathed a sigh of relief.

"You will find everything you need at her office in town. I will contact her secretary and let her know you will be taking over at least for the time being."

"Thankyou Richard it's the least I could do. Cybil was more than a friend to me and I am more than happy to help out anyway I can."

Richard looked over to Blake, he could see his Son was itching to go and he need to make a move himself.

"Blake could you see Olivia out, I will just let Dotty know what's going on then I too have to leave."

"Sure Dad." Blake escorted Olivia to her car.

She turned quickly before Blake could move away and kissed him on the lips, "I'll always be here for you Blake, if you need anything, anything, at all let me know. I will visit Cybil everyday and give you a report on how she's doing."

Pushing Olivia away he stated, "That's not necessary Olivia, both Dad and I will be checking daily with her doctor and visiting her." Blake started to back away. Checking his watch he said, "I've got get going, catch you another time." Walking away as fast as he could without making it too obvious he wanted to get away. Olivia smiled, she was in. She would make damn sure hers and Blake's paths cross regularly, she wasn't letting go this time not without a fight.

CHAPTER 14

MICKIE AND THE police officer were already at the shop when Richard and Mike arrived. In the light of day the extent of the damage looked a lot worse than the night before. People were in cleaning the message off Mickie's office wall and removing the rubble. Richard walked around the shop his anger growing, if Cybil had a hand in this destruction she would pay, even if that meant she would go to jail. He spoke to the Officer in charge of the investigation. Officer Peters show Richard and Mike the crime scene photos. They were both appalled; this was definitely a personal attack, except for stock being thrown around nearly all the damage was centred in the office.

Mike grabbed his clip board and measuring tape and started making notes; Mickie and several others were picking up the strewn clothing. She bundled it all up into boxes, the local dry cleaning company would pick them all up this afternoon and have them back to her by the end of the week.

Richard organised food to be delivered, when it arrived they all sat down and ate, it was then Mickie asked how his reception went when he got home.

"Blake and Cybil were arguing when I got in and of course once she saw me she went on the attack, then something happened and she ended up having some kind of seizure."

Concerned Mickie asked, "Is she going to be okay?"

"The initial prognosis isn't good, Doc thinks she's had some sort of meltdown, he is going to do tests so we will know more by the end of the week."

Mike joined them and put his proposal to Mickie, "What we need to do is fortify your office, can you close for the rest of the week?" Mickie nodded.

"Good I'll get a crew in to rebuild the office out of steel; we'll put in a secure phone line and electronic lock on your door, if you need anyone to have access we can scan them in. I would like to use reinforced glass in the windows to stop any smash and grabs. I've added an upgrade to your alarm system as well as surveillance cameras."

Mickie was taken aback with all the measures Mike wanted in, "Is all that necessary?" she asked.

Mike looked to Richard, "Yes Sweetheart, especially if you are here on your own or with Dylan I wouldn't rest easy if you didn't have adequate security."

Officer Peters agreed, "Ms Sullivan you don't know if this is an isolated incident, better to be safe than sorry."

"Mickie no one will know of the changes everything will look pretty much the same, we will use covert cameras, place them where no one will see them. Your office will look exactly the same except for the scanner on the outer wall." Mike tried to reassure her.

The bell over the front door chimed Mickie turned to inform the customer that they were closed when she noticed it was Rachel, her part timer; she had forgotten to call her.

Rachel stood frozen in the doorway, Mickie called out to her but she didn't respond, so she got up and walked towards the door.

"I'm sorry Rach I meant to call you and I forgot." Mickie apologized.

In a tiny voice Rachel asked, "What happened?"

"Someone broke in last night." Mickie watched as Rachel started shaking.

Concerned Mickie asked, "Rach are you okay?"

Tears slowly rolled down her cheek, "Oh god Mickie I think this is my fault."

Mickie put her arm around Rachel's shoulders and directed her to the table where they had been eating lunch; she poured a glass of water handing it to Rachel.

"Now tell us why you think this is your fault. Did you have something to do with it?" Mickie enquired gently.

Rachel shook her head, "No but I think I know who did."

Richard asked, "Can you give us a name?"

She nodded again, "His name is Barry Tibbs. He's my ex-boyfriend. He is involved with some very bad people, a couple of weeks ago while he was away on a business trip I found a bag stuffed under my bed, it was full of drugs so I flushed them down the toilet." Mike and the Officer Peters whistled.

"He went ballistic when he came back and couldn't find them, I told him I had flushed it all down the toilet, he lost it then and nearly beat me to death. He said there was twenty-five thousand dollars worth of drugs and that I would have to find the money to pay his employers or they would kill him. I told him I didn't have that kind of money, he told me to ask Mickie for it or steal it, I refused and he started threatening me. Everywhere I went he would show up and start abusing me, he rammed the back of my car last week that's when I went to the police and had a restraining order placed on him."

Everyone at the table realised the message on the wall had been personal but targeted at Rachel and not Mickie, that had everyone breathing a little easier.

Office Peters ask for a description and his address, Rachel gave it willingly. He called the station to organise a warrant for the arrest of Tibbs.

Mickie tried to comfort Rachel, "It's okay Rach and this isn't your fault. You can't help who you fall in love with."

Rachel nodded, "Mickie he was wonderful at first, and I thought I had found the man of my dreams. Then I think he started using the drugs he was selling and he completely changed. He became aggressive, moody, would sleep all day and stay up all night, he was always at some party or another. I grew tired of that life pretty quick and wanted everything to go back to the way it was but I guess he like it more than me, that's when he started hitting me. I knew I had to get away I was so frightened he would eventually kill me, I've been staying at a woman's shelter for the last week so he hasn't been able to find me I guessed he took his frustrations out on you Mickie, I'm so, so sorry."

Mickie hugged her friend, "Don't worry Rach a few things were broken, nothing was stolen and there's just a mess to clean up.

I'm closing the shop for the rest of the week so I can get it fixed up, so why don't you take the rest of the time off and get sorted out, call me on Friday okay?" Mickie walked Rachel to the door, hugging her again.

Officer Peters informed them that an 'All points bulletin' was out on Tibbs and patrols had been increased in the area in case he came back, he left soon after promising to keep them updated.

Mickie rang Kathie to see if Dylan could stay over there a couple of days explaining what happened, she said she would be happy to take him for the week if necessary but Mickie said she only needed a couple of days.

Richard and Mike left shortly after, Mike to organise the new office and equipment and Richard was heading to the hospital.

The rest of the day Mickie tried putting the shop back together, while taking a break she decided if they were going to redo her office she might as well give the rest of the shop a makeover. Grabbing her book and pencil she jotted down a few designs finally picking the one she liked the best, started making phone calls, by the evening she had everything organised. Builders would be in the following morning to start the new refit.

CHAPTER 15

RICHARD CALLED INTO the hospital before going to the office catching up with Doc Addams.

"Hi Peter, do you know anymore on Cybil's condition?"

"Yes Rick and it's not good I'm afraid. During the fit she had a severe stroke; she is paralysed down the left side along with that she had a small embolism which I suspect caused the seizure which in turn caused the stroke. She can't speak, I'm not sure if she even comprehends what is being said, her condition at the moment is in a vegetated state. She is currently on fluids through an I.V."

Even though he didn't love her anymore, Richard wouldn't have wanted her to end up like this, "Is there any chance she will return to normal function?"

"The damage is pretty extensive, she's had heart and brain trauma and as its early days the symptoms could worsen over time. I think you should resign yourselves to the fact she may never come home or resume the life she had before. I have seen patients with fewer injuries not recover. She will need constant care for the time being. There is a clinic I can recommend, 'Lady of Angels Hospice' the quality of care is exceptional and I can check in on her daily."

Richard nodded, "Okay Pete, can you organise her transfer and whatever else is required and just send the bills to my office."

Peter thought something major must have happened.

"Rick do you know what could have triggered this?"

"I'm not sure Pete, over the years Cybil had grown to be a very bitter woman, she tried to control things, tried to create this perfect little world where she was the Queen, then when reality started to crumble at her walls I think she realised she was losing everything and just snapped. She had become an angry violent person over the last couple of years and her mood swings would leave you dizzy. I did wonder if she had a brain tumour, I think the bitterness, anger and hurt eroded any goodness or tenderness in her. What is really sad Pete is she could have had so much if she had just let go of her jealousies. She has a wonderful grandson who will never know her or her him, a beautiful loving daughter-in-law and she threw it all away for what, to end her life like this."

Doc Addams sympathized, he remembered Cybil as a teenager she was pretty and came from one of the wealthy families in the district. He always thought her a bit odd, they had gone to school together would but she would only associate with people from a similar wealthy status. She wouldn't have given him the time of day back then, but once he became a physician and than a specialist in the field of neurology he was then fitting the standard she would place on those she associated with. Rick was right it was a sad ending to a life that had so much going for it.

"Alright I'll see to her transfer, it will possibly happen later in the week as long as her condition doesn't deteriorate any further."

"Thanks Pete, let me know if you need anything further."

Richard left the hospital and headed for the office, even though some people may consider his next course of actions cruel under the circumstances, he still intended to proceed with the divorce.

CHAPTER 16

ACROSS TOWN BLAKE had entered the Births, Deaths and Marriages registry office, he had called earlier and the information he requested was waiting at the front counter for him. He took the documents out and read their contents he was astounded and ecstatic at the same time. Seems his Mother had tried to push his alleged divorce through but some astute clerk had declined it due to incomplete paperwork and as it had his and Mickie's addresses on the documents she would never had known that the divorce hadn't been processed. He had not given it another thought when he didn't get the final decree, he was angry with himself for not noticing sooner and he suspected Mickie hadn't bother looking too much into it coming so soon after she had just lost her Dad.

He called his father to meet for lunch he couldn't wait to tell him what he'd uncovered, he left the registry office and as he was walking back to his car he ran into Olivia.

"Well hello there handsome," She greeted him.

His "Olivia" was said in exasperation, not that she noticed.

She asked, "How's Cybil?"

"I haven't heard anything further Dad saw the specialist this morning and I'm about to meet him for lunch."

She really wasn't very good at reading body language as Blake's was screaming, 'Get the hell away from me'.

He kept moving to his car and to his astonishment she invited herself to lunch.

"That sounds lovely; you don't mind if I join you then we can both find out how Cybil's doing together?"

Before Blake could utter a word she was seated in his car doing up her seatbelt. Great that's all he needed, his news would have to wait; he was not going to discuss his findings while she was there.

Richard sat at the table in his favourite restaurant and was surprised to see Olivia walk in with Blake; he made eye contact with his son only to have Blake shake his head.

Richard stood as Olivia approached the table greeting her, his upbringing forbidding him to just sit there. "Olivia"

She returned the greeting, "Richard. Blake said you might have some news about Cybil."

They all sat down as the waiter asked for their order, giving it Richard answered her question, "Her specialist is keeping her under observation for the time being he will know more in the morning." He only gave her the basics of information; he feel it relevent to discuss his wife's medical problems with someone he considered a waste of space. He had never liked Olivia James, thought her shallow, always looking out for the next poor sap that was richer than the last to further her bank balance. Now it seemed she had her eye set on Blake, he knew his son wouldn't fall for the likes of Olivia not after having someone like Mickie.

"Oh how dreadful, she will need extensive physiotherapy; I can be of great help there as I studied physiotherapy in college. Massage is a must as is muscle stimulation, the sooner it starts the better, the less wastage the sooner she will be on her feet again."

She chatted through most of the meal, both Richard and Blake were glad to see the end of it, Richard returned to the office and Blake took Olivia back to car before going to his father's office, then he would go and visit his Mother.

Blake apologised as he entered his Father's office, "Sorry about Olivia Dad, she just invited herself I wished to Christ she would leave me alone."

"I don't think that is going to happen anytime soon Son, your Mother has been grooming her for years to take Mickie's place."

Blake scoffed, "Like that will ever happen. What did Doc Addams say about Mother?"

"Unfortunately it isn't very good, he thinks she had a brain embolism which in turn caused her to have a stroke also she is paralysed down the left side, Pete isn't confident that she will regain full health. He is keeping her overnight to keep an eye on her condition then transferring her to a hospice where she will get twenty-four medical care." Richard thought now was the best time to tell Blake his intentions.

"There is something else I need to tell you, I have petitioned to divorce your mother."

Blake had been expecting this for years and wondered why his father hadn't done it earlier, "Does Mother know?"

"Yes and as you would have expected she went ballistic, maybe I should have done it years ago and then at least she may have had a chance of finding some happiness."

Blake sympathized, "I did wonder if you would ever sever the ties and find someone else and Dad I don't think anything would have made Mother happy, she was a very bitter short sighted person. She could have had so much only to end up paralysed and depending on someone to look after her basic needs it's such a sad waste of life."

Richard agreed, "Yes it is. Now did you found out anything at the B.D.M. Office?"

"Yes it seems Mother and some shonky lawyer did try to push the divorce through but apparently the paper work wasn't completed properly and it was never processed so Mickie and I are still legally married. Now all I have to do is find her and hopefully she will let me explain everything to her."

Richard encouraged his son, "Well don't give up Blake."

"Oh I don't intend to and if she has someone else I will fight tooth and nail to win her back." He assured his Father.

Richard smiled, "That's the Hunter spirit, never give up on something or someone worth the fight."

Blake smiled back, "I'm off to visit Mother and tell her the good news I just hope she can understand me."

They said their goodbyes and Blake left.

Cybil was in a private wing of the hospital, when Blake entered the room it was filled with machines buzzing and whizzing, there were multiple tubes in her arms and one up her nose. He moved to the bed and reached for her hand, it was upsetting to see her like this but she had created all these problems on her own.

"Mother can you hear me?" He looked at her open eyes for some kind of response but didn't see any. He sat down beside her bed.

"I'm not sure if you can understand what I'm saying or if you can even hear me but I am very angry at you, today I found out the truth. You failed in your attempt to separate Mickie and me; we are still legally married the divorce was never processed. Your solicitor falsified documents and our signatures, so I'm going to sue his ass and with a little luck get it thrown in jail. The unfortunate part is that you will undoubtedly be implicated as I don't think he's the type to take all the blame no matter how much money you paid him. I love you because you're my Mother but I don't like you very much. You could have had so much Mother but you let jealousy, hatred and envy destroy you. I feel so very sad and sorry for you because you will never hold your grandchildren, watch them grow, never know their love." He watched her face for any kind of sign that she either heard him or understood what he's said; he saw a tiny movement in her cheek, this was encouraging.

"Mother I will find Mickie and we will have a life together and I would have dearly loved for you to be part of that life but I see now that will never happen. I know why you have been pushing Olivia James in my face and even if she were the last woman on this earth I would still have nothing to do with her. Even though Mickie and I are married I intend to marry her again and have the family we always wanted and then I will move us as far away from you as I can get. I wish it could have ended differently but I don't want my children to be subjected to your bitterness, hatred and poison. I'm sorry you were unable to love Mickie and be happy for me, I dreamed of having a big family, with you the matriarch teaching your grandchildren the proper etiquette, helping then grow into productive members of the community now they won't have that and you will be left with an empty home, filled with silence instead of the laughter of children. Dad will be in later, he told me about the divorce." Blake shook his head, "You could have had so much Mother but you threw it all away to end up with nothing." He stood up to leave, "I hope you can understand or at least hear me Mother I will call in and see you when I can but I am making Mickie my priority." He kissed the top of her head, "Goodbye Mother."

Turning away he didn't see the tears slowly weep from her eyes or her eyelids gently close.

CHAPTER 17

MICKIE WAS THRILLED at how the new renovations were turning out. The new display windows were divided into four different compartments and each one had a carousel with three sections. She had placed mannequins in each and dressed them in varying garments. The first one was beach wear; it showed bikinis, shorts and all- in-one bathers; the second was day wear, the third evening wear and the forth naughty night wear. The compartments were painted with the appropriate scenes, the fourth had fairy lights placed in the roof to simulate a romantic starry night, she was please with the overall effect.

Mike had finished the office and even placed a concealed door at the back so she could exit the building without going through the front door. This made her happy as she didn't like walking through the side alley; it gave her the creeps having to go through it late at night to get to the deserted car park at the rear.

She had sectioned off areas in the shop with coloured sheer curtains turning them into 'Theme Rooms', there was a 'Goth' room where every bit of clothing and accessory was black, then there was the "Red' room were everything was red or had red in it. She had a 'Bridal' section with everything white and lacy, then the dress up area that held nurses, policewoman, French maids and dominatrix outfits for those more adventurous.

Mike had placed some lovely artwork around the shop which also concealed the surveillance cameras, external camera were also place outside the building, no one was getting in here without being seen.

Upstairs still remained the store room and Dylan's play room, Mike had added ornamental bars to the windows with sensors in several corners as well as cameras, not that anyone could access the top floor without a large ladder or lifting devise. He had given her a stylish pendant and a bracelet that she wore during the day, if she felt threatened at any time she was to depress the centre stone to activate the alarm system that would alert police and the security company.

Kit had been in several nights to help her in the store, he didn't like her being there alone especially at night with Tibbs still out there. Mickie called Rachel and asked if Tibbs had been in contact but she had gone to her family's home and he didn't know where they lived, she gave Mickie her new mobile number as she was paranoid that Barry would be able to trace her by the old one.

It was Friday and all the stock was now in the shop, Mickie put up 'New Reno Grand Opening' sale signs in the windows and on a sandwich board outside the shop. She had hauled some old stock from the store room downstairs and put it in the seventy percent discount bins, it was time to have a good clean out and make room for the next season of stock.

The door bell over the door tinkled, Mickie looked over and saw Kit checking out the finished look.

"What do you think?" she asked nervously.

Kit whistle, "Very impressed, love the 'Themed areas' especially this one." He held up the dominatrix outfit with furry handcuffs and a whip made out of satin cord.

"I can just see you in this; care to try it on for me?" He wiggled his eyebrow in hopeful anticipation.

Mickie scoffed, "Dream on sweet cheeks you will never see me in that or any other of those outfits, they're a little too gaudy for me." Mickie laughed at Kyle's disappointed sad face. "Don't worry I'm sure one of your many 'lady friends' would gladly parade around in front of you wearing that."

Kit put the garment back, "You need to kick back and be a little daring my love, it would open up a very big world out there if you did."

"Thanks but no thanks, I like my life just as it is. I don't need the world to see what should be for my husband's eyes only, or go to every party and flirt with every available man in sight. There are names for girls that do that I should know my Mother-in-law has called me just about everyone of them."

Kit curiosity got the better of him, "Why does Cybil Hunter hate you so much?

Mickie sighed, "I had the audacity to fall in love and marry her precious son; a girl from the wrong side of the tracks, coming from a blue collar family with no money, I was good enough to be his 'Whore', her words", she explained at his gasp, "but not his wife. Cybil had already chosen who she wanted to marry the Hunter Prince and when he refused to concede to her demands she blamed me and has hated me every since. Mind you her determination is to be admired; she tried her hardest over the years to break us up finally succeeding about three years ago when he divorced me. So I have seen that side of life and it leaves me cold so you can have your 'Dolly birds' I'll stick to plain old boring."

Kit reassured her, "Sweetheart that is one thing you are not, you're just a little conservative, which is a refreshing change from as you say the 'dolly birds' always looking for a rich husband and using their bodies as collateral. In fact it makes you that much more desirable knowing that delectable body hasn't been seen by all and sundry."

Mickie blushed. It always embarrassed her when he commented on her looks.

She looked like such an innocent when she blushed.

"So are you just about finished?" he enquired.

Tidying the counter she asked, "Nearly why?"

"Well, I thought I might take you and Dylan out for dinner then go and visit the circus in town."

Mickie smiled, "Dylan would love that. I'm just about done; I'll pick him up and head home. Can you give me an hour?"

He checked his watch, "Sure I'll meet you at your place at say five thirty." He waved as he walked out the door.

Mickie finished up, set the alarm and locked the back door. She turned around and was horrified to see her car. Every window had been smashed, every panel had been damaged and her tyres had been slashed. Red paint had been poured all over the car, shaking she looked around at the now empty car park there was no one in sight. Turning, she quickly unlocked the office door and rushed inside. Grabbing the phone she immediately called the Police and Mike. Mike told her to secure herself in the office until he arrived.

Mike was there within ten minutes, he called Mickie on her phone and she unlocked the front door and Office. First thing he asked if she was ok and checked the rest of the store to make sure it hadn't been breached, he then went out to check her car.

Whistling at the sight of the damage Mike realised this guy needed to be caught and quickly before this escalated any further.

Re-entering the office he went and checked the dvr, (digital video recorder), there was Tibbs in living colour trashing Mickie's car, Mike put a disc in to record the whole attack, the police would be wanting it to press charges if they ever got to catch the freak.

Officer Peters arrived with a Detective Johnson as did the scenes of crime crew; they started immediately on the vehicle while other officers combed the area in case Tibbs was still hanging around.

Mike showed them the footage and gave the Detective the copy he made; he also made one for himself. He contacted the security company to get extra patrols on the premises. He also called in some of his boys, they would stake out the shop over the weekend in case Tibbs returned.

Officer Peters organised a tow truck to remove Mickie's car to the police holding yard once Scenes of Crime had finished with it. Mike got one of the boys to bring over a company car for Mickie to use until she got her car back.

Mickie was still shaking after the police had left; Mike could see she was in no condition to drive home, he offered to pick up Dylan and take them home.

Mickie was really scared now. Tibbs obviously couldn't take his anger out on Rachel so she was now his target.

"Mike what if he knows where I live, he could hurt Dylan?"

Mike tried to reassure her, "If it's ok with you I would like to station one of my men at the house and I will have some of the boys keep an eye out over the weekend. Don't worry Mickie my guys won't let anything happen to you or DJ."

They picked Dylan up from Kathy's place Mickie tried to act as normal as possible she didn't want to frighten Dylan; she was seriously considering sending him away until Tibbs had been apprehended.

"Hi Mike." Dj greeted his Grandfather's friend.

"Hey Bud, how was school today?" Mike greeted Dj back.

Dylan wasn't curious about Mike being in the car as he had been picking him up from school quite often lately.

"I didn't like it much; today the teacher made me sit next to Sally Rogers, she kept touching me and giggling all the time. Mike girls are really dumb." Mike laughed knowing that attitude would change in about ten years.

Mickie couldn't let that pass without comment, "Hey there mister girls aren't dumb."

"I didn't mean you was dumb Mum, you're not a girl."

Raising her eyebrows at Mike, she was afraid to ask.

"I'm not huh, so what am I?" she couldn't wait to hear what he had to say.

"You're just Mum."

Both Mike and Mickie laughed. Some of Mickie's tension eased.

Dylan looked quizzically at them both not understanding the joke, grownups were such weird people.

Kit was waiting for Mickie when she got home, he was concerned when he turned up and she wasn't there.

Mike pulled in the driveway beside Kit's car, he opened Mickie's door and one look at her face he knew something was wrong.

"Hey you ok?" he asked.

Mickie shook her head motioning to Dj and mouthed 'tell you later'. He helped her out of the car, nodding to acknowledge Mike.

"Hi Kit, are you going to take Mum out?" Dylan greeted Kit

"Hi Dj", he returned the boy's greeting. "Well I was hoping you might want to come too. There's a circus in town I thought we might go and get something to eat and go see it."

Dylan turned to his Mother excitedly, "Can we go Mum?"

"Sure Baby why don't you go and get changed."

Before he went inside Dylan asked Kit, "Do you like girls?"

Kit looked at Mickie and Mike, "Is this a trick question?"

Mickie shook her head holding back a laugh, her son asking the biggest playboy in town if 'He liked girls'.

"Sure Dj. Don't you?"

"Nah they're dumb, all they do is giggle and keep touching you, and they talk funny." He grumbled

"Give it time Mate, some get better as they get older." He ruffled Dj's hair.

Dylan shook his head, "Nup I'm gunna stick with my mates at least they aren't afraid of worms." Dylan waved goodbye to Mike and headed into the house.

Kit turned to Mickie, "So what's going on. Why is Mike bringing you home?"

"Tibbs trashed my car at work."

Kit was concerned, "When? Not when we were in the shop?"

"Seems so, the police have taken my car to their holding yard. The car is a complete write off, Kit this man is insane."

Kit wrapped his arm around Mickie's shoulders offering comfort and support, he looked over to Mike.

Mike answered Kit's unasked question, "I've got guys out here and at the store and I'm placing one in the house until this guy is caught. The police are doing extra patrols as is the security company, we'll catch this bastard."

Kit looked down at Mickie, she didn't deserve this and if he ever got his hands on this guy there wouldn't be a lot left to identify. He couldn't tolerate men who thought women and children were there for them to take their frustrations out on; they were the type, he knew from experience, that never stood up to another man.

"We don't have to go out if you don't want to?" He said quietly.

"No I think it would be good to go at least I won't be sitting inside wondering when he will strike and Dylan will love seeing the circus."

Just then Mike's ride pulled in behind Kit's car, he said his goodbyes and left.

Mickie and Kit entered the house, Brandon; one of Mike's men had secured the rear doors and windows by placing sensors on them connecting them to her existing alarm system, if they were broken or breeched the whole neighbourhood would hear about it. Dylan and Mickie showered and changed in record time, while he waited for them, Kit helped Brandon set up the sensors.

Mickie instructed Brandon to help himself to the fridge and cupboards for food and drinks before they left.

DJ chatted the whole way to the restaurant all through the meal and on the way to the Showgrounds where the circus had set up; they could hear the animals call into each other when they got out of the car. There was a carnival type atmosphere with fairy floss machines, trinket stores, food stalls and rides for the children to enjoy. Kyle bought tickets for Dylan to go on the rides. Dylan rode the merry-go-round and on the jumping castle before they entered the big tent, to be entertained by clowns, performers and animal acts.

D.J. was thrilled to be picked to help the Clown put out an imaginary fire with a confetti water cannon. He was enthralled by the trapeze act and the animals, even getting to hand the elephants and apple each. By the end of the night they had one very tired and happy little boy.

Mickie thanked Kit for a wonderful night, not once had she thought of Barry Tibbs and his terror campaign. He offered to spend the night on the couch, Mickie declined not wanting Mike's staff to get the wrong idea about their relationship.

Mickie was waving Kit off when the telephone rang.

Mickie answered, "Hello"

"Hello Sweetheart, Mike just told me what happened to your car are you okay?" Richard asked concerned.

"Hi Rick, yes I'm fine it just put the wind up me a bit, this guy has a major problem and I hope the police catch him soon. I'm seriously thinking of sending Dylan away until this guy is caught, if anything happened to him I would never be able to forgive myself."

Richard agreed, "Maybe Dylan would like to come to the cabin for a couple of weeks of fishing and swimming with his grandad?"

Mickie thought that was a great idea but was concerned especially with Cybil's medical condition.

"That sounds great Rick what about Cybil?" She enquired.

Richard was always humble by Mickie's compassion, for everything his wife had done to her; Mickie still put Cybil's needs before her own.

"Unfortunately Cybil's condition had deteriorated, she fell into a coma two hours ago and the prospects of her coming out of it are slim according to the doctors. She is getting the best medical care there is, they have moved her to the intensive care unit and will be under constant supervision. I am only a phone call away and a couple of hours drive if necessary. I think it will do both us boys the world of good to get away."

Mickie had to ask, "Will Blake be going with you?" Wondering how Richard would explain Blake's presence to his son.

"Would you like him to?" Richard queried

"No, I think I should be there when Blake meets his son for the first time, just in case Blake rejects him."

Mickey's heart squeezed at the thought of Blake turning his back on DJ, it would break her son's heart to know his father didn't want him.

"That's fine Sweetheart I understand, then it will just be DJ, his grandad and a security team spending some quality time together."

"Thanks for understanding Rick and I know DJ will love to spend the time with you and the boys."

They made arrangements for Richard to pick up Dylan in the morning first thing. It was a weight off Mickie's mind to know that her son would be safe and far away from the threat of Tibbs.

CHAPTER 18

DYLAN WAS BESIDE himself with excitement waiting for his grandfather, Mickie had explained that they would be spending two weeks together at the cabin, fishing and swimming and doing all those boy things Dylan loved. Dylan loved the outdoors and had always loved the cabin; he was out the door before his grandfather had stopped the engine.

"Grampa, Grampa; are we really going to the cabin for two whole weeks?" He asked excitedly.

Richard ruffled Dylan's hair, "We certainly are champ. Do you have everything you're going to need packed?"

"Sure do Grampa. When can we go?" He was so excited he could hardly keep still.

"As soon as you give Mummy kiss goodbye, we're out of here."

Dylan ran to his Mother's side, pulling her down for a goodbye kiss.

"Bye Mum." He dashed off towards his grandfather's vehicle climbed inside, put on his seatbelt and waved to his mother out the window.

Mickie laughed and waved back blowing her son kisses. She was happy he was now out of harm's way.

Tibbs snorted another nostril full of white powder, his habit was getting out of control, he realised this because he was watching one of his dealers slowly bleed to death in front of him from the knife wound he had just inflicted. The idiot had tried to sell him the crap he dealt to the dopers on the street. He had paid for premium grade cocaine and what this fool tried to give him was little more than baby powder. Nobody gets away with ripping him off. What was really pissing him off was the fact that he couldn't locate that whore Rachel she seemed to have disappeared, that bitch was going to pay dearly for costing him so much money and reputation. He didn't know if she had any family or where they would be, maybe he should have listened to her instead of banging her every chance he got. He was hoping that rich bitch of a boss would have bailed her out; now with Rachel out of his reach he would have to get his money from the next best thing, her boss!

Tibbs was proud of the damage he had done to her car he hoped it would shake her enough to cough up the money; he would leave it a few days and then make contact. He gathered his bag full of contraband and left the dingy squat, someone would eventually find the rotting corpse.

Mickie kept busy throughout the next couple of days, one of Mike's men drove her in every morning and one was positioned outside the shop at all times. Customers loved the new renovations and sales were up, she contacted an I.T. expert to set up her internet online web store and from the response in the last couple of days it looked very promising.

Richard let her know they had arrived safely at the cabin and Dj was getting their security team to build him a fort. The bell over the door tinkled, Mickie looked around to welcome her customer, her smile dwindling when she recognized Olivia James.

Olivia sashayed into the store like someone of importance; it irked her that Mickie had made such a success of her business ventures. She knew Mickie also held a substantial real estate portfolio and that she was respected in the business community as an astute business woman. Olivia's money came from all her ex-husband's bank accounts; she wasn't cut out to work for a living especially not as a shop keeper.

"This looks very nice Mickie," she complimented

"Thankyou Olivia, is there anything in particular you were looking for?"

"Why yes," she cooed.

I want something sheer and very sexy." She picked a red negligee from the rack and held it against her body; there were red stockings, suspenders and a red g-string that went with the outfit. Mickie had recently added glamorous stiletto shoes to her inventory; she knew the outfit would look sensational on Olivia with her colouring. Olivia must have agreed as she purchased the lot.

"Someone will be in for a nice surprise when he sees you in this." Mickie complimented her on her choice.

"Yes I think Blake will be very pleased." Olivia watched for Mickie's reaction.

Mickie hesitated wrapping the garments for a second, "Blake?"

Olivia tossed her hair back, "Yes, I'm sorry didn't you know he was back?" feigning concern.

Mickie continued wrapping, "Yes I was aware he had returned."

Olivia then stuck the knife in, "Yes he's been back for nearly a week now, as I'm sure you are aware that my marriage has ended."

Mickie interrupted, "Is that's number three or four I've lost count?" Then she felt ashamed for being so spiteful.

"It's my third husband; anyway we now have something in common and have been consoling each other also with what has happened to poor Cybil he has been beside himself with worry and leaning on me for support. He has also asked that I take over managing Cybil's charities until she is well enough to step back into the fold." Mickie showed no reaction, so Olivia struck a little deeper.

"Plus it won't be long before he asks me to move into the house. With Cybil so sick he will need someone with experience in these things to take over the running of the household, hosting their dinner parties and any corporate events."

Olivia was such a bitch but Mickie knew for certain she wouldn't be moving into their house not if Richard had any say about it, and it was obvious she hadn't heard of Cybil's deteriorating condition.

"Really what does Richard think of this, you moving into his house and all?"

Olivia waved her hand in the air like she was brushing away a fly, "Once I am in there he will see what an asset I can be, organising parties and so forth."

"So Richard doesn't know that you plan on moving into the house?" Mickie pushed.

Now Olivia was feeling a little cornered, "I'm sure Blake will win him over and really the house is so big we would barely run into each."

Mickie had to ask, "So Blake intends to stay?"

Olivia laughed, "Of course silly, where else would he want to live especially now with us reuniting and with his mother being so sick." She checked her watch, "Ooh I must fly, Blake's meeting me at the hospital we are going to visit his mother together."

Well that didn't take Blake long; back a week and already hooking up with his mother's protégé. Blake had always said that Olivia was a waste of space he must have changed since he's been gone to consider hooking up with Olivia. What she said cause Mickie to experience a multitude of emotion from anger to hurt and finally a sadness filled heart. Deep down inside her hidden away was the last bit of hope she had that one day they would be a family, it bought her to tears to think that Dylan would never know his father. She knew Richard would never let Olivia move into the house as it was his and not Blake's; she supposed Blake would be looking for a place of his own. It was going to be hard to see him around town with Olivia and any children they had, she decided then that she would not tell him about DJ, Mickie knew that it would cut Dylan deeply that his father didn't want him but had a family with somebody else. She gave herself a mental shake, wiped her eyes and got back to work.

CHAPTER 19

IT HAD BEEN two weeks since the incident with Mickie's car she had sent it away to have a G.P.S. tracker and an alarm system installed, she was starting to feel Tibbs had given up when the phone rang.

She answered and Tibbs greeted her with, "Hey Bitch, like what I did to your car, if you don't pay me the money that whore stole it won't be your car I smash up it will be your pretty face."

Mickie hand was shaking; she hit the duress button around her neck and Damien, one of Mike's men flew in the door she handed the phone over to him, he hit the record button put it on speaker so they could all hear what was being said.

"You listening to me Bitch! You got three days to get me my Twenty five grand otherwise I will take it out on that body of yours."

Damien mouthed for Mickie to keep him on line long enough for them to trace the call.

Mickie stammered, "Who is this? I don't know what you are talking about."

"I'm the guy that bitch Rachel stole from and I want my money back."

"Rachel doesn't work here anymore she quit weeks ago, if she owes you money then you need to speak to her."

"Well there's the kicker, I can't find her." He all but screamed down the phone making Mickie take a step back.

"So tell me where she is and I'll go get it from her, if not you better come up with it!"

"I'm sorry I don't know where she is, she said she was going interstate to be with her family and I don't know where they are." Mickie stalled hoping they traced the call quickly.

'You must have her number?" Tibbs knew Rachel had cancelled her old number.

"No I don't, the one I usually call her on, has been disconnected."

Tibbs snarled, "Well looks like you are gunna have make good on her debt now don't it? I will call back in three days and tell you where to drop it off and you better have it and you better not call the cops or you're gunna be in a world of pain and that little boy of yours might end up an orphan."

Now Mickie was angry, he shouldn't have threatened Dj, "You listen to me you rotting piece of garbage, there may have been a very slight chance I might have paid up but seeing you just threatened my son you can go to hell. If the police don't get you I might just find out who your bosses are and let them know YOU stole their drugs let's see how long you out last then."

Damien signalled they had the trace and the police were on their way as she spoke, he encouraged her to keep him talking.

Tibbs spat back, "Bitch you do that and I will guarantee you'll end up in a box, I will burn your house and your business to the ground." He laughed evilly, "And just for good measure I might even blow your car up, so don't you ever threaten me again Whore cos you will come off second best. Now just get ME MY MONEY and wait for my call." Tibbs slammed the phone down.

Mickie was physically shaking she had never been so scared in her life, Damien helped her to a seat, "You did good Mickie." He praised her; he poured her a glass of water, handing it to her.

"God I hope they catch that guy he is totally insane, Mike came through the door then rushing to Mickie's side.

"Are you ok?" She was pale and shaking.

"Yes, please tell me you guys got him?" She looked up at Mike.

He didn't want to scare her anymore than she was but she needed to know the truth, "Unfortunately he was gone by the time the patrol car arrived don't worry they will get him Mickie be assured of that. Is there any chance you could close the shop for a while until he is captured?"

"Mike I've only just reopened from his last attack." She was shaking her head.

Mike understood, "How about we put someone else in here to run it while you go to the cabin with Dj and Richard." He saw she was going to refuse, "Mickie do it for Dj if not for yourself, remember what it was like to lose your Mother so young, do you really want to put him through that?"

Mickie's eyes filled with tears, "That's low Mike."

He knew he was being cruel but it was only because he was concerned for her life, "I know Mickie and I'm sorry for stooping so low but Richard would tar and quarter me if anything happened to you and for now that is the safest place for you to be."

She agreed, "OK Mike, I know you're right but please catch this maniac as quickly as you can."

He breathed a sigh of relief; she would be out of harm's way while they set about capturing this bastard. "We will."

He promised. "The police will have an undercover officer pose as you to do the drop and they will pick him up then."

It was nearly closing time so they decide to close up early, first thing in the morning Damien would take her to the cabin; an extra team would be dispatched with them just in case Tibbs had a way of tracking Mickie.

CHAPTER 20

MICKIE AND HER team left bright and early the next morning, she had spoken to Richard the night before and he whole heartedly agreed with Mike. She rang KIT and let him know she would be out of town for a week or so, he offered to go with her but she gracefully declined.

Meanwhile Blake had tracked down the solicitor his Mother had used, to say Mr Dwayne Atkins was surprised to see Blake standing in his office was an understatement. Blake studied the man in front of him. He was a pot bellied unkempt scruffy looking fellow, his suit had seen better days and his office looked like it had been ransacked. At the same time Atkins was positioning himself behind his desk for a little protection, he knew of Hunter Senior's reputation and looking at the man in front of him the son hadn't fallen far from the family tree.

Clearing his throat he enquired, "Can I help you?"

Blake continued to stare at Atkins, "I won't introduce myself as I'm sure you know exactly who I am; I'm just here to inform you that I have started legal proceedings against you, not only will you lose your license but I will guarantee you get a prison sentence."

Atkins knew this day might come but he took the chance anyway, the money Cybil Hunter paid him was far too good to pass up but he did have an ace up his sleeve.

Leaning back in his executive chair he said, "Well if I go down so will your Mother; she hired me to do it so she is as guilty as I am." He knew the son wouldn't want to ruin his good Mother's reputation. He had a smug smile on his face.

Blake took the wind right out of his sails, "That's fine I have informed my Mother that you would probably implicate her to save your own neck. The thing is she will state she only asked you if it could be done. There are no documents with her signature on it giving you approval to pursue, lodge or falsify any documents. She will say she never authorised you to harass myself or my wife into signing those illegal documents and yes she did pay you a considerable amount of money but she would say that you were blackmailing her and really it's the word of a washed up highly disreputable solicitor against someone to whom is held in the highest regard within the community. Have a guess at who the courts will believe?"

Atkins knew he was sunk, "So what do you want?"

"Me nothing but the police waiting in your foyer would like you to go with them." Blake gave him a satisfied smile.

Atkins took one last swipe, "You are one cold hearted bastard you know that, just like your father."

Blake laughed, "I'll take that as a compliment. I've at least done the community a service by getting rid of corrupt scumbag like you." Blake turned and walked out of the office while the Officers handcuffed Atkins.

Blake decided to join his Father at the cabin it had been years since he was last there. He went to the hospital to check on his Mother, her condition was getting worse. When he got there the doctors were debating on whether to intubate her as she has stopped breathing several times during the night. Blake made the decision for them and told them to go ahead and do it, he would inform his Father and he would have the final say on whether to retain it or remove it when he got back.

Peter Addams spoke to Blake, "You need to prepare yourself for the worst. Cybil's condition is deteriorating rapidly; her brain activity is slowing that is why she stops breathing."

"How long do you think she has?" Blake was sadden his mother was slowly slipping away.

Pete gave him the truth, "With her now being on life support, for as long as it takes or until someone turns off the machines, she's comfortable and not in any pain."

Blake nodded, "I'll be seeing Dad tonight so I will tell him. Can you do me a favour and stop all visitors unless otherwise instructed, especially Olivia James. We don't want it getting around town how sick Mother really is when the time comes we will decide what to tell people,"

Pete agreed, "I'll inform the staff immediately, the intensive care unit only allows immediate family anyway."

Blake nodded, "That's what I figured but I know Olivia will try and pass herself off as family to get in to see her."

Peter assured Blake she would have no access.

They shook hand and said goodbye.

Blake went home to inform Dolly she could have a couple of weeks off as he would be joining his father at the Cabin and if Olivia called she was to be told he had gone out of town for a few days.

CHAPTER 21

DJ WAS SO excited when his Mum arrived she had barely got out of the car before he was dragging her off to see the fort they had built. She was surprised at how big it was, there a rope ladder that could be pulled up so the enemy couldn't get in, a veranda surrounded the whole fort and a lookout tower was mounted on top with a telescope to check the horizon. It was a very impressive structure big enough for four adult men to stand inside and move about comfortably. Two bunk beds lined one wall and looked like they were being used by some of the boys even though the Cabin had eight bedrooms. There were chairs and a table plus a sink and tap with running water. The windows had shutters and protective screens, the door had a dead bolt and there was a trap door in the floor for a quick getaway.

DJ asked if he could sleep out there with one of the boys, Jerry assure her he would be safe so she agreed.

After the evening meal Richard, Mickie and some of the guys were sitting down having a drink, Dj was sound asleep in his fort when the call came a vehicle was approaching the cabin, all of Mike's men went on alert. Mickie and Richard were secreted in a room at the rear of the cabin while Mike's boys found out who their visitor was. Mickie was terrified, had Tibbs somehow tracked her to the cabin, had she put all their lives at risk?

"What about Dylan?" she stammered.

Richard put his arms around her, "Sweetheart he'll be fine Jerry and Ryan are with him."

A few moments later Damien released them from the room.

Richard asked, "Who was it?"

Damien smiled and moved aside so they could see who it was.

Mickie's heart nearly stopped in her chest, Blake had come to the cabin.

Blake stood there not uttering a word he was in shock at seeing his wife standing before him. He had been looking for her for a week and she had been at the cabin the whole time and his Father knew.

Richard broke the extended silence first, "Blake I didn't know you were coming up here."

Blake answered his father without taking his eyes off his wife.

"I thought I would join you and give you an update on Mother's condition but I see you already have lots of company."

Mickie excused herself and went to her room without speaking to Blake.

Blake turned on his Father, "You knew she was here all along?"

"No Son she arrived this morning unexpectedly." Richard knew Blake wasn't about to let Mickie's presence here go without some explanation.

"And what's with all the security? I was all but stripped searched what's going on? Are you in trouble?"

"Have a seat and I will try to explain. Mickie's business was broken into and threats were made, the person who did it owes money to a drug cartel. He was dating one of

Mickie's staff members who had since left and because he can't find her he is trying to extort the money from Mickie. He trashed her car a couple of weeks ago and yesterday gave her a threatening phone call. Mike and the police thought it wise to get Mickie out of the way while they set up a sting operation to capture this man, so she was packed up and sent here with a security detail just to be on the safe side."

"Do they know who this freak is and why didn't you tell me?" Blake was angry now; his father should have told him Mickie was being threatened.

"Yes but so far he has eluded the police they intend to pick him up when he goes for the money and honestly Blake it's Mickie's business and she didn't want anyone to know."

Blake was stunned, "Mickie isn't going to pay him is she?" Richard shook his head, "No, an undercover officer is going pose as Mickie; the bag will be filled with fake notes in case he checks."

Looking towards Mickie's closed door he asked, "Do you think she will talk to me?"

"Does she have a choice?"

"Dad you know we have to talk. I had that lawyer arrested today; he said he was going to implicate Mother. I told him if he did he would also be charged with blackmail, I guess we will have to see. I spoke to Doc Addams as well, Mother's been put on life support he said he will discuss her further treatment with you when you got back."

Richard nodded, "What do you think we should do Blake?"

Blake gave his Father his honest opinion, "It may seem uncaring but I think she should be able to die with dignity and not be kept alive by machines, that's not what I would call living."

Richard agreed, "Yes you're right, I will see to it when we get back."

Meanwhile Mickie was wearing a hole in the bedroom floor pacing madly, chewing on her finger nail. Blake turning up so unexpectedly had put her right off kilter; she was going to have to tell him about Dj tonight because when morning came it would be too late.

When the knock came she knew it was him, taking a deep breath she opened the door.

His wife took his breath away she had grown more beautiful if that was at all possible. "Hello Mickie."

Her "Blake" was said barely above a whisper.

"Can we talk?"

She stepped back to allow him entry into the room.

Mickie left the door open and went to sit on the bed; Blake pulled the chair out from the corner.

"How have you been?" He so wanted to grab her up in his arms and hold her like he used to but he knew he would need to take thing slowly he didn't want to scare her off.

"I've had better weeks, you?"

"Yes. Mickie there is so much I need to tell you I just don't know where to start.

"I find the beginning is always a good place." She knew this wasn't going to be easy and she wasn't going to like what he had to say but it was better to get it out in the open now. She was a much stronger person than the simpering mess he left behind all those years ago so whatever he said she would deal with it.

CHAPTER 22

"FIRSTLY I AM so very sorry to hear about your Dad, I loved him like he was my own father and if I had known he was ill I would have been back here in a shot."

Mickie gasped. "Your Mother said she told you but you were too busy to come home."

"Yes well I have since found out a lot of things my Mother has said and done without my knowledge but we will get to that later. I want to apologise for the way I left, for not being man enough to face you in person and hope that one day you can forgive me."

Mickie saw the sincerity in his face and heard it in his voice, softly she asked, "Was it because of me, did I make you unhappy?"

Blake felt like a real bastard all these years she thought it was her fault he left, "God no Mickie, please don't ever think that. I know I should have discussed what was going on but I thought I could deal with it myself only I couldn't and took the coward's way out and walked away. I realised after a few weeks that I had left the only good thing in my life behind, I tried to call you but there was no answer. I told Mother that I was coming back to get you that's when she told me you had left the same day I had, put the house up for sale and she didn't know where you had gone."

Mickie was furious, "She's a liar, your Mother threw me out of the house after trying to claw my face off, she knew exactly where I was as did your father. If it wasn't because of me then why did you leave?"

"It was a multitude of things, I was sick of the pressure Mother was putting on me to join the firm and her constantly throwing her friend's daughters at me. Steve had presold a dozen copies of the program I was working on that was constantly crashing and I saw the disappointment on your face every month you got your period. I guess I felt like a failure and thought a fresh start would fix everything only it made it worse. I missed you so damn much and when I tried to get in contact there was no answer. I did call Dad's office but they said he had taken a leave of absence, I even tried your Dad's number but it had been disconnected."

Mickie remembered it so clearly even now, Richard was staying with her and her father at that time; he had turned off his mobile phone because Cybil was constantly calling.

"Dad had to do it because your Mother was calling constantly day and night screaming abuse down the phone; she only stopped when Richard told her he would get a restraining order put against her if she continued with the harassment."

"Mickie I am so sorry she did that to you, you didn't deserve it then or when we were together. Dad explained a few things to me regarding Mother but that's not to excuse her for what she has done. Can I tell you why she was like she was?" Mickie nodded.

"Her biggest problem was jealous firstly of your Mother and then of course you. I'm not sure if you know this but Mother was in love with your Dad but because of his background her parent forbid her to have anything to do with him."

Mickie was shocked, "Are you serious? Dad never said anything about an affair with Cybil he did say they had a history, I thought he meant because he worked for Rick."

Blake continued, "I'm not even sure there was a relationship. If her parent had the slightest suspicion she was interested in him they would have put an end to it. Mother was groomed to marry well it would have been an embarrassment to her family if she had wed beneath her standing. When Mother and Dad married I guess George realised he and Mother had no future, then he met and fell head over heels in love with your Mum. It ate Mother up to see him so happy with another woman and one so popular. Your Mum was a beautiful person inside and out she was always there to give a helping hand; nothing was too much trouble and it didn't matter if you had a million dollars or one dollar. She volunteered on most committees especially for the homeless and handicapped people, some of those Mother was also on but she always came in second fiddle to your Mum that's when the poison set in and continued to the end."

Mickie now understood some of Cybil's animosity, "When Mum died I would have thought that would have been the end of it, why did she turn on me?"

"That was my fault, I fell head over heels in love with you and she could see history repeating, another woman taking away someone she loved." He reached over and held her hand. "And I still am to this very day."

Mickie pulled her hand away, "Really Blake; you expect me to believe that? Olivia James came into my shop the other day and told me she was moving into the house and that you and her were together and besides that you divorced me remember?"

Damn Olivia, he thought she might try and sabotage him by carrying on his Mother's vendetta to make sure Mickie wouldn't take him back. He would make sure Mickie knew exactly where he stood with Olivia.

He would put her straight right now, "Firstly Olivia and I are not and never will be together, in fact I can't stand the woman and secondly I didn't divorce you, you divorced me!"

Mickie stood up starring down at Blake, "Are you crazy, I never did, ask your father if you don't believe me. It nearly destroyed me receiving those papers I thought we would be together forever and always. I burnt the first lot you sent me and I didn't sign the second ones for months. Your damn lawyer rang me every day for over three months in the end I gave in and signed them; I'll admit I was really peeved with you that I tore up your damn cheque but I DID NOT INSTIGATE THE DIVORCE!" she shouted.

Blake stood, "Sweetheart I know you didn't and neither did I." He waited for the penny to drop.

Then it dawned on her, she looked up at Blake shocked, "It was Cybil?"

He nodded, "Yes she hired a corrupt lawyer he filed the papers forged our signatures and if it hadn't been for a very observant clerk they might have succeeded." Blake waited for the information the sink in, it took a moment then she said, "Are you saying we are still married?"

Blake nodded, "Is that going to be a problem?"

He was concerned now in case she was involved with someone else.

She pushed him away, "Yes damn it, it is. I had finally resolved myself to the fact that you were never coming back and decided to get on with my life."

"Does that mean have you met someone?" he demanded.

Defiantly she raised her chin, "What if I have! Don't forget you walked away from me Blake, left me behind. Did you expect me to wait until you decided you wanted a wife again, to stay single for the rest of my life pinning for your return?"

Pain pierced his heart, he knew it was his fault but it angered him to think another man was holding his wife making love to her as he had. He turned away so she couldn't see how much her words had hurt. But she had.

Taking a deep calming breath she said, "Look Blake it's been nearly six years and not once in that time have I heard a word from you, if you wanted to you could have found me but you really didn't put too much effort into it with or without your Mother's interference. I'm not the same woman you left all those years ago."

He agreed, "You're right it is my fault and yes I should have put more effort into finding you but when the divorce papers came I kind of lost it for a while and buried myself in work. It was only when Steve offered to buy me out I realised how lonely my life was, how empty inside I had become and I didn't want to be that person anymore. You were the only one that every made me feel alive, gave my life some purpose."

She thought now would be a good time to tell him about Dylan.

"Blake I have responsibilities now and they come before me and my wants and needs."

"Do you mean your shop?" he asked.

"No Blake it's not the shop or my real estate holdings, it's my son."

Blake felt like he'd been hit with a sledge hammer, she'd had someone else's baby; the knowledge nearly crippled him. He staggered back to the chair he needed to sit down.

"You had a baby, is the father still around?"

She became evasive, "His father left before he was born."

"Does he know about the child?" He needed to know especially if he wanted her back in his life.

"No, when he left he said he didn't want to be a father so I didn't bother to tell him." She was hoping that would ring some kind of bell in him.

"If he knew he might have come back." He knew he would have.

"I was hoping he would come back to me on his own I didn't want him back just because I was pregnant."

"Do you intend to tell him at all he has a child?" Even though the child wasn't his he would adopt him and raise him as his own if Mickie would still have him.

"I'm sure he will figure it out sooner or later." She answered quizzically.

Blake looked at her oddly, "Are you saying he lives in town?"

She guessed he wasn't real quick picking up her subtle hints.

"He does now." She thought she might have to hit him with a lump of wood to get her message across.

God what a mess first he leaves then some guy gets her pregnant then he too leaves and both he and this guy return at the same time.

It was like being hit by a lightning bolt, she was talking about him.

"Mickie are you saying we have a son?"

"Took you long enough, Yes Blake we have a son."

"When were you going to tell me?" He demanded

"I just did." She pointed out the obvious.

"You know what I mean Mickie, would you have ever told me?"

She shrugged her shoulders, "I don't know Blake, maybe. Look Dylan's welfare is my main concern, Olivia told me you two were together and I wasn't letting that bitch anywhere near my son."

Blake could understand her reluctance to have Olivia anywhere near Dylan she definitely wasn't good with children. "Mickie I swear to you on my life, Olivia means nothing to me, never has never will. Does she know who Dylan's father is?"

"Yes Blake she knows you're his father as did your Mother but she chose to ignore his existence. She told all her friends that I had an affair which was the reason you left me because I wouldn't abort my boyfriend's 'bastard child'. That's probably why no one told you of his existence before now."

"Does my Father know?" He thought if anyone would tell him it would be his Father.

"Of course Richard knows, he and my father supported me through my pregnancy and Dylan's birth, he's been there from the start. I don't think I would have made it without his help especially after Dad got sick, Rick would babysit while I took Dad to hospital and his doctor's appointments. I should also tell you that during that time your father stayed with us for a few months. Some people assumed we were having an affair and that Dylan was possibly his but I can assure you he isn't."

"I suppose you are the 'Whore' my Mother refers to that Father spent all his time with?" It was all clicking into place now his Mother's over the top reaction when his Father got back home.

Mickie nodded, "Yes that would be me." She wanted him to know how she felt about Richard.

"Blake I love your Dad like he was my own and it disgusts me people would think so little of him to accuse him of such behaviour. I can understand it of your Mother because she has always hated me but it angers me that members of the community snigger behind their hand speculating."

"You know my Father wouldn't care less and was probably flattered that people think he could pull someone as beautiful as you." Blake knew without a doubt his Father wouldn't have done such a thing.

Mickie smile, "Yes he has mentioned that."

Blake braced himself before he asked his next question, "Mickie am I going to meet our Son?"

Her spine straightened "That depends, when you left you said you didn't want to be a father and I don't want Dylan thinking he was the cause of you leaving, I won't have you hurt him."

It saddened him to have her think he could hurt an innocent child, "Mickie I would never make him feel he was to blame." He assured her.

"Good then we better come up with a story as to why you haven't been around since his birth because he is going to want to know."

Blake was pleased if he could win his son over maybe, just maybe he would win Mickie over and they could be a family.

"So where is he?" Blake asked.

"He's close; you will meet him in the morning." Mickie yawned it had been a long emotional day and Dj would be up with the birds.

Blake could see how exhausted Mickie was, "I better go so you can get some sleep. Mickie I would like us to spend some time together with and without Dylan can we do that?"

Mickie thought for a moment, "For what purpose Blake?"

Blake knew this wasn't a conversation for now and just said, "Because I've missed you." Without another word he left the room closing the door.

Mickie was so tired, her encounter with Blake hadn't been as traumatic as she has expected, seeing him again she realised she still had strong feelings for him and they needed to be sorted out before she made any decisions on her future, there was also the fact that they were still married. She hoped the police caught Tibbs real soon she needed to get back to some normality.

She crawled under the covers and was asleep before her head hit the pillow.

Richard was waiting for Blake as he exited Mickie's room, "How did it go?"

"Ok I guess, Dad why didn't you tell me I had a son?"

"It wasn't my call Blake. Mickie had been so traumatized by your leaving and from Cybil's attack; she was angry, scared and hurt, your note said you didn't want to be a father so she took you at your word. She swore that if George, Dolly or I broke our promise and told you she would leave."

"She said Mother knew about him."

"Yes she knew. Dylan was over at the house with Dolly when your Mother came home early one afternoon, she went ballistic in her usual Cybil manner scared the life out of poor Dj, he must have been about three, she told Dolly Mickie's 'bastard son' was never to be allowed in her house again. It wasn't long after that George had his first heart attack so I moved out and in with Mickie to help her with George and Dylan."

Blake shook his head, "I'm glad you were there for them. Mother never said a word in all those phone calls, about Mickie or George and definitely not about Dylan."

"She knew you would come straight back if you knew Mickie was pregnant or had your child, that wasn't on her agenda for the two of you to get back together, she preferred people to think he was my child than have you find out. So what do you plan to do now?"

"To get to know my son and wife again, she agreed to spend time together"

"How did she take it when you told her you were still married?"

"As you would expect shocked, then angry, she didn't tell me but Dad is she dating anyone?" He needed to know.

"Well I don't know if you would call it dating but she has been spending time with her accountant, Kyle Anderson. He has taken her to a few charity events and took Dylan to the circus the other night I don't know how serious they are. I know he hasn't spent the night at her place, I don't know if she has been to his when Dylan has been away if that's what you are asking."

"Why does he go away?" Blake frowned.

"He goes camping and fishing with Mickie's friend Kathy and her family and has sleepovers there; he gets to mingle with other kids and Mickie gets a break, with the shop being open five and a half days a week she doesn't get much time to herself."

Blake nodded and looked at the time, "I might hit the sack myself I'll see you in the morning Dad."

Ok." Richard watched as his son left the room he hoped Blake and Mickie could make a go of it he loved them both dearly and wanted them to be happy.

C H A P T E R   2 3

MICKIE KNEW DYLAN would be up as soon as the sun broke the horizon, Jerry and Ryan kept him busy until they saw signs of life in the cabin. Richard was getting things ready for breakfast when Dylan bust through the door.

"Ahh…. Grandpa I thought I might be up before you,"

"Well Lad I think you might have been by a minute or two, now what do you want for breakfast?"

Richard simultaneously spoke as Dylan gave his order, "Crambled eggs with bacon and lots of cheese."

Dylan laughed, "Grandpa if you know'd what I was gunna have why did you ask me?"

"Just checking that's all." While Richard got busy cooking Dj's breakfast Blake arrived in the kitchen.

Seeing his son for the first time was heart stopping, Dylan saw him and said 'Hi' without blinking an eye, he was obviously used to strangers being around, then he asked, "Do you want Grandpa to cook you some crambled eggs with bacon and cheese, that's what he's making me?"

Richard turned from the stove to see Blake starring at his son; there was a look of total amazement there on his face, he knew Mickie wouldn't be happy as she wanted their first meeting to be with her present. As soon as he thought it he looked up and saw Mickie watching the encounter from the doorway.

"Morning Sweetheart coffee?" he greeted her. She nodded, Blake still hadn't moved from his spot watching Dylan.

Mickie didn't want to disturb the scene in front of her. Blake seemed mesmerised by their son, Dylan noticed her then.

"Hi Mummy, do you some of Grandpa's crambled eggs?"

"Hi Baby, yes that sounds lovely." Mickie moved to sit beside Dylan. Dylan asked in a stage whisper that everyone could hear, "Mummy, why does that man keep staring at me? Does he know how to talk, cos I asked him if he wanted cramble eggs and he didn't say anything, is he one of Mike's men?"

Mickie smiled, "Yes Sweety, he knows how to talk and no he isn't one of Mike's men." She wanted to explain Blake's appearance as simply as possible to her son.

"You know how you are my son?" He nodded.

"Well Blake is Grandpa's son."

"Is he here because the wicked witch isn't living at Grandpa's house anymore?" He asked.

Mickie knew exactly who Dj was referring to, she chastise him for referring to Cybil as a witch, "No Dylan and it's not nice to call your Grandmother a witch, Blake's been away for a long time and has just come home."

DJ turned to look at the man, he seemed familiar like he had seen him before but couldn't remember where, then it dawned on him, he was in a photo Aunt Dolly showed him and he was hugging his Mum.

Dylan's next question had everyone gasping, "Do you know my Daddy?"

Blake looked to Mickie for an answer.

She asked, "Honey, what makes you ask that?"

"Cos I member Aunt Dolly showed me a picture of him and he was hugging you, is he your brother Mummy?"

"No Dylan he's not my brother" she didn't want to explain who Blake was to Dylan in front of all Mike's men so she said, "How about you wash up for breakfast and we will talk more about it after we've all eaten."

"Okay." Dylan ran off to wash up telling his Grandpa not to forget the cheese as he passed.

Mickie helped set the table for everyone to sit down to eat, all Mike's boys came in from their night shift and the morning crew were up to start theirs. Dylan was seated at the head of the table next to Mickie and chattered to everyone nonstop throughout the meal. After everyone had finished Dj wanted to go exploring and asked if anyone wanted to go, his security detail of four men put their hands up, he told them they were going to look for a pirate's cave and see if there was any treasure in it.

Mickie told him he had to be back by lunchtime as he set off with is fellow explorers.

CHAPTER 24

MICKIE AND BLAKE settled on the swing on the front veranda, "You've done a wonderful job with Dylan Mickie and after everything my Mother has done to you, why did you still stick up for her?" She had a forgiving soul, if it was the other way round he didn't think he could be so generous.

"Don't pat me on the back too hard Blake, I think your Mother is a right royal bitch but I won't have Dylan disrespecting his elders no matter how evil they are. You know she could have moulded him the way she wanted you to be, he could have been the new "Hunter Prince" but she tossed him to the kerb and for that I will never forgive her but she is still his Grandmother and he will show her respect."

"Dad said she was pretty nasty to him when he was at the house."

"Yes and sadly that is how he will always remember her. He was scared after that, frightened the wicked witch was going to come and steal him out of his bed in the middle of the night. For weeks he slept in my bed and I can tell you if our paths had have crossed I would have punched her out for frightening a little boy like that."

Blake felt terrible; it was because of him his Mother had turned on Mickie and their son, "I'm sorry Mickie for everything." Mickie studied her husband; he was as handsome as ever and he still gave her butterflies but his face had a sadness to it that wasn't there before he went away, his eyes had lost that mischievous twinkle, he seemed more serious.

"Blake what are your plans now that you are back?" she asked.

He wondered what her reaction would be if he told exactly what he wanted but he settled for the basics. "I am taking time off work for a while, I want to reconnect with my Father and hopefully be a part of yours and Dylan's life if you will let me."

Her life had all of a sudden become complicated; she wished the past had never happened.

"I guess we will have to take it a day at a time, get to know each other again. You hurt me so much when you left Blake, if we decide to make a go of it and it won't be for Dylan's sake, you better be damn sure you're in for the long haul because if you walk away again it will be forever."

He breathed a sigh of relief taking her hand in his rubbing his thumb over her knuckles, "Mickie believe me I have no intentions of ever walking anywhere unless you are with me. I deeply regret all the hurt and pain I have caused not only you but your Dad and my family and I promise to always discuss things with you so that we can jointly make the decisions that will affect us as a family."

She needed to tell him of her burgeoning friendship with Kyle she didn't want any misunderstandings between them.

"I need to tell you something, I have been seeing someone casually for a little while. I have known this man for a number of years and it's only recently that, to put it simply we have been dating."

Blake felt a stab in the region of his heart. "Is it serious?"

"For Kyle it probably would be in a heartbeat but I'm a bit more cautious these days and I have DJ to think of. He's a good kind man," she smiled.

Blake didn't like that.

She continued, "He also has a bit of a reputation as a playboy." Blake definitely didn't like that.

"What does Dylan think of him?"

"He likes Kyle just fine I guess, loves Kyle's car more though, he's a typical boy."

"Do you think he will be a problem?" Blake would fight tooth and nail to protect Mickie.

"Kyle? Be a problem in what way?" she asked.

"I don't know maybe try and talk you out of any relationship with me, try to keep us apart?"

"I know he will, not just for himself he knows how Cybil has treated me, he has seen it first hand and he wouldn't want to see me hurt like that again. He's a lot like you used to be, a bit over protective."

"Do you think I should have a talk to him assure him of my intentions?" He would put Anderson straight on a few things but mostly warn him off, Mickie was his and he will do anything to keep it that way.

"No I will tell him about you, he's been a good friend and it would be a little crass having my ex-husband do it."

"You mean husband." Blake corrected her.

"That will take a little getting used to." She looked out over the hillside.

"What did you do with your rings" He was curious, his wedding ring hung around his neck on a chain.

"Ahh… Well your Mother took those from me as they were apparently family heirlooms." She rubbed her finger where Cybil had pulled the rings off.

Blake guessed by the way she was rubbing her finger hadn't been done with any pleasantries.

"I'm sorry I will get them back to you she probably has them in her jewellery box."

"If it's all the same to you I really don't want them back, don't take this the wrong way Blake but I feel those rings are cursed and they are best left where they are." Even though he had given them to her, they had belonged to Cybil's family and she wanted nothing to do with them.

He understood where she was coming from. It had been his Grandparents that had really started it all by denying Cybil the man she loved but then if they hadn't they would never have been born, fallen in love and had a son.

"Maybe when we get back we can go looking for a new set?" He thought he might put his idea forward while they were on the subject.

"Mickie when you are ready and this is only if you want to, would you consider remarrying me?"

She looked at her husband suspiciously, "For whose benefit?"

He held up his hand in innocence, "Just ours honestly. I just want to delete the past and make a fresh start, a new life as a family. Dylan could carry the rings and Dad could walk you down the aisle."

"Let me think about it ok?" she said. She didn't think she was ready to take that particular step yet.

"Sure I promise not to pressure you, if I do just tell me to back off." He smiled.

She had loved his smile and that twinkle was back in his eyes.

They saw Dylan coming over the ridge, they must have been sitting there for hours just talking it was old times. Mickie realised all the tension had left her body. She decided that for the rest of the time they were at the Cabin she would enjoy with her family.

DYLAN CAME BACK disappointed they hadn't found a pirates cave but he had collected a lot of strange things to add to his collection.

Everyone had lunch and Blake asked Dylan if he and his mum would like to go for a swim in the lake, they went and got into their bathers and headed to the water.

On the path to the jetty Blake asked Mickie, "When are you going to tell him I'm his father?"

"Soon," she promised.

They had been swimming for an hour when everyone got back on the deck, Dylan turned to Blake, "Are you going to live in Grandpa's house with Aunt Dolly and the w…. nasty lady?"

Blake smile, his son was quick to fix his near slip giving his mother a quick look to see if she heard.

"Yes for a little while but the nasty lady isn't there at the moment so if you every want to come and visit your Grandpa and Dolly you can come anytime."

DJ shook his head "I betta not cos sometimes she comes home and no one hears her and then she starts screaming really load and says lots of bad words, she is really scary."

"It's ok Dylan she won't ever scream at you again I promise." He assured his son.

"So how come you was away so long?" DJ asked.

"Well I wasn't very well so I left until I got better." He didn't know how much to tell a five year old that he could understand.

"Okay." His acceptance of Blake's explanation astounded him he took it on face value.

"Do you know Mummy's friend Kyle?" When Blake shook his head he said, "He has the coolest car and it goes really, really fast and Mummy says he has lots of girlfriends. Do you have lots of girlfriends?"

Blake shook his head, "No I don't. Do you have any?"

Dylan response made Blake laugh, "Ewww no way girls are dumb, they giggle all the time and want to touch you and they don't like getting dirty or playing with bugs and worms. I don't know what they are good for or why there are girls. They can't build forts, they don't go fishing or hunting, they ain't got much use hey?"

Mickie had been quietly listening to their conversation but she couldn't let DJ get away with that.

"Excuse me a minute there Mister chauvinist piggy, who washes your clothes, cooks your meals, picks up after you Hmm?"

Dylan frowned, "Who is Mr Piggy?" totally confused.

"You are, didn't you just tell Blake girls are good for nothing?"

"Girls don't do those jobs silly, Mummy's do." Dylan said logically

"So what are Mums if not girls?" Blake couldn't wait to hear his son's answer.

"Mums are different to a girl that's all." Dylan explained. "They can do much betta things than girls and they don't mind getting dirty and you can tie Mums up, betcha a girl won't let you do that!"

Now Blake was intrigued, "You tie your Mum up Dylan?"

He looked over at Mickie and raised his eyebrows, had she developed a kinky side he didn't know about.

Mickie met his eyes and blushed knowing exactly what Blake would be thinking.

"Sweetheart, tell Blake why you tie us up?"

'Us?' this was getting more interesting by the minute.

"Mum and Aunty Kathie let us tie them to a chair when we play cowboys and Indians, we have to rescue them before the train comes and smooshes them. Then we have to catch Uncle Greg, he's the bad Indian that ties up Mum and Aunt Kathie then he gets tied to the chair. I don't know why but Aunty Kathie giggles a lot when she does that, I think Uncle Greg must be telling her a joke."

Blake had a fair idea what Uncle Greg was suggesting to Aunt Kathie and he couldn't' wait to meet these people.

"See it's all very innocent, not at all what you were thinking."

"Sweetheart all I was thinking of where the times we could have used some of that rope."

Mickie blushed to the roots of her hair, good thing her son didn't understand what they were saying.

"I remembered you liked the outdoors, even this deck holds many a fond memory."

Mickie knew exactly what he was referring to. They had spent the night on the deck with a blanket and body heat to keep them warm. They had made love most of the night and as the sun broke over the horizon it was a magical moment one that obviously neither had forgotten. Even now she could still remember the feel of his naked body against hers, his mouth and hands seem to touch her everywhere, they were so hot for each other she thought they may go up in flames.

One look at Blake's face she knew he was thinking of the same night when he softly said, "One day I hope we can do that again."

The sexual tension between them had been building all day Blake thought he might disgrace himself when Mickie took off her shorts and t shirt, her bikini was bright yellow and was the sexiest thing he had ever seen. Her body was tanned and showed no traces of her pregnancy accept maybe her bust looked bigger but then she always had a sizable chest for someone with such a slim build.

Mickie had been doing her own covert inspection, it looked like Blake worked out regularly his body was ripped, he had a six pack and his biceps were huge. She remembered those arms holding her so tenderly, carrying her over the threshold of their new home, cradling her close to him after one of his Mothers verbal attacks. She knew it would be so easy to fall back into them but she had to be sure this time was forever because it wasn't just her, she had Dylan to think of.

Blake could feel Mickie's eyes caressing his body it made him hotter than ever, he decided to take Dylan for a swim to cool the embers so as not to embarrass himself in front of everyone.

He hoped he would last the week without dragging her off to the bush to have his wicked way with her, he knew if she paraded around in that bikini too often his resolve wouldn't last.

They stayed on the dock for a couple more hours then went back to the cabin; Richard had set up a barbecue on the deck for the evening meal.

CHAPTER 26

MIKE HAD RUNG Richard and informed him the sting operation would take place the next day, everything was in place. Tibbs had made contact and the drop zone was to take place in a vacant industrial estate. Mike thought it a strange place for a drop as it was very secluded and away from the general public. It would make the police's job in capturing him that much easier and with a lot less risk, with a little luck Mickie could be back home by the weekend.

Richard asked Mike to advise him as soon as the coast was clear.

The morning of the drop Mike, four of his men and six officers as well as the Mickie decoy arrived early at the site, they set up surveillance to alert them of Tibbs arrival. Unbeknown to the police officers, Mike and his team Tibbs had been there the day before and rigged the place with explosives he had no intentions of letting that rich bitch identify him to the police he was damn sure there would be no witnesses.

The time of the drop approached and the teams were alerted to Tibbs arrival everyone kept undercover leaving only the officer impersonating Mickie standing between the two factories. As Tibbs had never seen Mickie he didn't know the woman waiting for him was a police officer.

"So bitch you decided to pay up, smart move on your part." He was looking her up and down, "Mind you I could definitely gone a few rounds with you horizontal, you're pretty little thing aren't you? Smart too not to involve the coppers." He looked down and saw the duffel bag.

"Is that my money?"

The officer said, "Yes," she slowly moved towards the vehicle, "If that's all I have to go."

"Hang on a minute Princess what's your hurry; I got to check the money first."

The comms in the officer's ear alerted her that the team was about to move in while Tibbs was busy counting his cash.

The first two layers were the real deal totalling about five thousand dollars the rest of the money was counterfeit.

When Tibbs was happy that the money was there he zipped up the bag and made his way to his car turning he pulled a gun out and shot out the officer's tyres. "Just so you don't get any ideas of following me."

He turned back to his car and saw a team of Police guns drawn heading his way he dived for his car as he was leaving he called out, "Bitch I warned you what would happen if you crossed me, you have less than a minute to get out of here before this place rocks."

All hell broke loose then the officers, Mike and his team ran for cover as Tibbs made his escape out of estate, he watched the explosion from his rear view mirror. That will teach her to cross him, he laughed, and he got the money and smoked the bitch as well as the coppers in one move.

He had to make a stop at the unit to grab his stash and some clothes he would drop the money off to his boss and get out of town for a while. He thought he had better count the money to make sure she hadn't stiffed him; he emptied the bag on the bed and started to count it. When he got to the third bundle he noticed the feel of the paper was different, he grabbed the previous notes to compare he realised quickly she had substituted counterfeits.

He roared, "Bitch you're lucky you're dead I'd kill you if you were still alive." He punched the wall.

He was in real trouble now, he was twenty thousand dollars short and he had already told his boss that he would have the money today. He took a snort to calm his nerves then another, he paced the room. What was he gunna do, what was he gunna do? His boss had warned him this was his last chance if he didn't have the money today he wouldn't be a problem tomorrow. Tibbs realised he was going to have to hit his dealers to get the money together, he separated the cash put the real stuff under his pillow and bundled the rest together, he would substitute the counterfeit stuff for what his dealers had at least it would give him some breathing space with his boss.

Meanwhile back at the industrial estate the officers, Mike and his team were brushing off the dust and debris; they had underestimated Tibbs he was smarter than they thought. There was nothing on his file to indicate he knew anything about explosives, now they understood why he picked such an isolated area. If luck was on their side Tibbs would think Mickie and the officers had been blown up in the explosion that gave them time to plan another assault.

The officer in charge alerted the station to the situation he ordered a team to head to Tibbs apartment and to approach with extreme caution he was armed and dangerous. By now they figured he would know that he had been duped so he would be looking to make up for the lost money. The police alerted all banks and money lending facilities that they could be at risk of an armed robbery. They faxed Tibbs photograph and general description of his vehicle to the banks and all law enforcement agencies, he was desperate now which made him extremely dangerous and to add to the mix high on cocaine made for an extremely volatile unstable person.

Tibbs contacted his dealers telling them he needed a big score and that he would be around shortly to pick it up, he went from house to house using the counterfeit money to buy the drugs then taking note of where the dealers put the money. He would head back later and take what he needed, his phone rang he answered, "Yeah what you want?"

"Why Barry, I want my money of course." The voice on the other end stated.

"Ah sorry boss didn't realise it was you." He stammered

"Do you have my money Barry?"

"Almost, just picking up the last of it now Sir." He lied

"That's good to hear Barry, so when can I expect to see you?"

Looking at his watch he said, "I'll be at the club by eight o'clock." He stalled for time that would give him five hours to collect the money.

"Okay Barry, eight o'clock it is but I warn you if you do not show up with all you owe me you had best leave town and go live in a cave because if I have to come looking for you there won't be enough of you left to identify, understood?"

"Yes Sir don't worry I'll have all your money and I'll be there by eight o'clock."

Barry went back and hit all his dealers taking not only the real ones but the counterfeit notes as well, they would come in use especially with him now having to leave town he would use them to get across the country.

Back at the unit Barry counted out the money he put his bosses in a red duffel bag and the counterfeits in the blue bag the bitch had given him, he was about to leave when his front door exploded.

Police officers stormed the apartment, Barry tried to pull his gun but the officers had him on the floor and handcuffed in seconds with Barry screaming the whole time. They collected the duffel bags, drugs and as much evidence as they could, Barry would be going away for a very long time.

At the station Barry was processed; his charges consisted of blackmail, extortion, drug dealing, possession of explosives and firearm offenses as well as assault and attempted murder of police officers to name a few, they had enough on him to lock Barry up and throw away the key.

While the detectives were interviewing Barry; an officer from the Organised Crime Unit interrupted calling the Detectives aside. He explained that they had been investigating Barry's boss who was suspected to be the Head of one of the largest crime families in the country, they would offer Barry a deal if he rolled on his boss. The detectives took it to their Captain, he was agreeable as long as Tibbs wasn't released back into the community at least not here, that he serve time for his crimes and when he was released he wasn't to step foot in Grayson because sooner or later he would find out that Mickie was still alive and that would put her life at risk.

The O.C.U. Officer agreed, he took the file and went to collect Barry.

The Captain wasn't real happy about the whole thing but if putting Tibbs out there caught a bigger fish then so be it but heads will roll if anything happened to Mickie Sullivan.

The Captain contacted Mike and let him know the outcome, Mike wasn't pleased that Tibbs could get a deal but was happy he wouldn't be in town. Mike rang Richard straight after the Captain's call and let him know it was all clear to come home. Richard sent most of the security detail home and left only a skeleton crew on at the Cabin, they decided to stay the remainder of the week. Mike organised one of the girls from the office to run Mickie's store until her return. All they had to do is sit back and enjoy their time together.

CHAPTER 27

THE WEEK ENDED far too soon for Blake, he could have stayed there indefinitely. He was getting to know his son and his wife again, his love for her was stronger than ever and this time it would be forever, he just needed time to prove he was worth a second chance, win her trust then her love.

Mickie too was disappointed the week had gone so fast, Blake's attentiveness to Dylan was fascinating to watch, he listen intently to what their son had to say, as though he was hearing the most important things in the world. Watching them wrestle and play together bought a tear to her eye she had never seen Dj so happy. She knew she would have to tell him soon that Blake was his father but she wanted him to get to know the man first.

First thing Richard and Blake did when they got back was go to the hospital to see Cybil; Doc Addams met them at the ICU, "Hi Rick; Blake." He greeted both men.

Richard's "Pete" and Blake's "Doc" said simultaneously.

Pete updated them on Cybil's condition, "It's not good she is now totally on life support there is nothing further we can do for her she has little brain activity, barely registering in fact so for all intense purposes she is brain dead. The machines are keeping her organs functioning in case you were wishing to donate any of them, she had indicated that she was a donor on her license but in the end it is up to you."

Richard looked towards Blake, "Would it bother you?"

Blake shook his head, "No if that's her wishes I'm all for it, if she can give life to someone else then do it."

"Ok Pete use whatever you need, I'll organise a media release and alert the funeral home." Richard looked at his wife she finally seemed at peace he hoped her next life was a happier one than this one had been.

They were both heading out the door of the hospital when they ran into Olivia.

"Hello Richard, Oh Blake you're back," she greeted both men. Turning to Blake she cooed, "You are a very naughty boy for not telling me you were going away, Dolly said you had a business meeting I hope it was successful?"

"Yes quite successful actually." He replied.

"That's wonderful. I tried to see Cybil while you were away but the hospital wouldn't let me, they said it was only immediate family. I tried to explain that I was family but they still wouldn't let me see her."

"But you're not family Olivia, you were only her friend." Richard stated.

"Really Richard we both know I was much more than that, I was the daughter she never had, she was like a Mother to me." Olivia wiped an imaginary tear from the corner of her eye. "Cybil was grooming me to take over her charities and fundraisers, ask her she will tell you herself."

"Unfortunately she is too ill to take visitors at the moment, so if you could keep running her charities in the meantime that would be much appreciated."

"Yes of course I will." Olivia agreed immediately.

"If you will excuse us we need to get home." Richard turned heading for the car Blake following close behind.

Olivia called to their backs, "Call me if you need anything, anything at all." If she didn't know better she would have thought they were giving her the brush off, maybe they were just upset at seeing Cybil so sick that could be the only explanation for their strange behaviour.

When he got home Richard informed Dolly of their decision, it brought tears to her eyes but it was for the best, having a machine breathe for you was no life and really for whose benefit were they keeping her around for?

Peter called and said the funeral home could pick Cybil up in a week, Richard organised for the funeral to be held in ten days time. He decided not to release her death notice until a couple of days before the funeral the last thing he wanted was her friends swarming to the house with their fake condolences.

Both Richard and Blake went to Mickie's place for dinner the following night; he wanted to let her know what they had decided.

Dylan opened the door to let them in, "Hi Grandpa." He jumped up into Richard's arms for a hug.

"How's it going Champ?" Richard returned his embrace.

"Alright I s'pose." He sounded a bit glum.

Blake asked, "Why so down Buddy?"

Dj looked at Blake, "Cos I have to go to school tomorrow."

He whispered overly loud, "Can you tell Mum I have to go back up to the Cabin with you, say its special men's business no girls allowed."

Before Blake could answer Mickie butted in, "I heard that Dylan James and no you can't go up to the cabin, you have to go to school you have already missed a week young man."

"But mum," he whined

"No but's, now go wash up for dinner." She instructed him, turning to Richard and Blake she said, "Come on through I'm just about to dish up."

They both followed her though to the kitchen, the smells emulating from there were mouth watering, Blake's tummy grumbled.

Mickie laughed, "Glad you bought your appetite."

Richard poured everyone a drink just as DJ joined the group, he sat next to Blake. Mickie brought the laden plates to the table, he had really missed her cooking, you could give her a box of food and she would turn it into the best meal you ever had.

Once the meal was finished and the dishes done Dylan went up for a bath and to get ready for bed, they had to wait until Richard had read him a story or three before they could talk.

Mickie was sad to hear of Cybil's passing; Richard asked if she wanted to attend the funeral she was about to decline when Blake asked her to go.

"Do you think that would be appropriate, given our past?" she asked.

"Why not, you are still her daughter-in-law." Blake stated.

"Yes but won't people think I have gone there to gloat?"

She pointed out what most of Cybil's friend would be thinking.

"Not the ones that know you and the others well they aren't worth worrying about." He really wanted her there at his side.

Richard stepped in he could see this was difficult for Mickie, "Honey if you feel uncomfortable about going there then don't go it's entirely up to you." He gave Blake a look that said 'Back Off'

"I'll think about it, what time will it take place?" She was still uncertain if she would attend.

"Next Saturday ten o'clock at Dempsey's Funeral Home."

"If I do come I won't bring Dylan, he might start chanting 'The Wicked Witch Is Dead,' I'll see if Kathie can have him for the night."

Blake laughed, "Don't reckon that would go down well with the fraternity."

Blake hoped she would be there not to snub her nose at his Mother's friends but to support him. He felt their relationship was moving in a positive direction. There were also selfish reasons on his part he wanted Olivia to realize there was no hope in her pursuing a relationship with him for he was well and truly taken.

CHAPTER 28

THE DAY OF the funeral was wet, cold and miserable. Mickie decided to attend the service against her better judgement. She had originally decided not to go but Blake had begged her to attend, she thought it would be petty to boycott her Mother-in-laws funeral and she wanted to show her support for Richard and Blake.

Mickie chose a grey satin suit with a pale pink blouse; she wore her mother's pearl necklace and earrings finishing it off with a pair of Victorian white lace boots. She looked elegant and quite regal, every inch a lady.

When Blake and Richard picked her up in the limo they were both taken back by her beauty not just her outside features it seemed to radiate it from her very being. Blake loved her so much; he knew how much this was costing her to stand in front of all his Mother's friends and he knew she was only doing it for him.

When she got in Richard asked, "You ok Sweetheart?"

She gave him a nervous smile. "Yes, but I will be glad when it's all over."

Blake reached across and took hold of her hand, "If anyone makes you feel uncomfortable you let me know."

She nodded.

They arrived at the church entering through the rear; Father Patrick greeted them at the door, he was the priest that married them all those years ago. He gave Mickie a hug, "It's nice to see you Mickie."

"You too Father, wish it was under better circumstances though." She returned his embrace.

"Yes but it all comes to us eventually." He said sadly.

He then addressed Richard, "I've put the family in the front pews and the rest of the congregation can sit where ever they want. I have kept the service short like you requested about half an hour, we can go over it if you like before everyone gets here."

Richard and Father Patrick went to his office to fine tune Cybil's eulogy while Mickie and Blake watched the church fill rapidly with Cybil's friends and associates. Mickie didn't see Olivia James but she doubted she would miss such an occasion.

The time had come for everyone to take their seats; Richard sat at the end followed by Mickie, Blake, Dolly and her family. Mickie could hear whispers everyone wondering why she was there no doubt.

Cybil's favourite music had just started to play before the eulogy was to begin when there were gushed whispers. Everyone turned to see who it was that had caused the commotion and unfortunately it was no surprise to Mickie to see it was Olivia; she had waited till the last minute to make her grand entrance.

What an entrance it was. It was not so much her being late that had everyone whispering but what she was wearing, to call it scandalous was an understatement.

The attire Olivia had picked for Cybil's funeral was the shortest black laced dress Mickie had ever seen with a plunging neckline nearly to her naval, she had obviously forgone a bra as Mickie couldn't make out any straps and her breast swayed as she walked. She had six inch stiletto heels and a hat almost as big as a sombrero that had a black veil hanging from it. The ensemble made her look like a porn star out of a Goth movie. She made her way to the front of the church giving Mickie a filthy look the closer she got. She stood in front of Blake and said, "Blake honey, can you ask her to move along so I can sit down."

Blake looked furious as did Richard.

Richard spoke first, "I'm sorry Miss James these are reserved for family members only you will have to take a seat somewhere else."

Mickie watched as Olivia's mouth opened and closed but nothing came out, before she could Richard spoke again, "Or you could just leave?"

The look she gave Mickie as she tranced off was nothing but pure venom, great another one continuing Cybil's hatred.

The rest of the service went off without a hitch, as they were loading Cybil's coffin into the hearse the sun broke through the clouds placing a bean of sunlight onto the coffin. As Mickie watched the light she thought 'He's showing her the way home'. She hadn't realised she had said her thoughts out load until someone said "That's a lovely thought."

Blake placed his arm around her shoulders kissing the top of her head, "I hope she can finally find some peace."

Everyone started to leave and make their way back to the Hunter home for the wake, Richard had been against it at first but Mickie said people needed closure and to talk amongst friends share their memories it let people say goodbye in their own way.

As they all climbed back into the limo Mickie could hear Olivia calling out to Blake. Pushing her way through other guests she asked breathlessly.

"Blake can I catch a lift back with you I caught a cab here and I don't want to hang around in this inclement weather."

Blake resisted in telling her to 'buggar off' and opened the door. Mickie and Dolly were already seated so when Blake entered she tapped the seat beside her for him to sit down.

The ride to the house took half an hour; Mickie wished she had taken the cab as Olivia talked non- stop most of the way.

Mickie could see that Dolly wouldn't be able to hold her tongue for too much longer.

Mickie turned to look out the window when Dolly asked Olivia about her clothing, "Girl what do you call that outfit?"

Olivia was taken aback by the question, "What's wrong with my outfit? It's the latest in designer clothes and costs a fortune."

Dolly raised her eyebrows, "Really well if you paid more than twenty dollars you were ripped off. You look like a two dollar harlot; if that dress got any shorter you'd be arrested for indecent exposure, plus someone with your size bosoms should wear a bra, you look quite trashy and I'm sure Cybil would be turning in her grave if she knew what you showed up to her funeral in. You must have had her fooled thinking you was a lady." Dolly looked at Olivia's feet, "Really you needed to wear those high heels and you're walking on toothpicks."

Olivia's face reddened either from anger or embarrassment Mickie wasn't sure, Olivia turned to Blake in a hope to muster some support.

"Blake darling, you don't think I look like a hooker do you?"

Blake didn't want to be brought into the discussion but had to tell her the truth, "Well it isn't what I would call appropriate attire to attend a funeral and those shoes are dangerous you could break an ankle." Now Olivia was getting mad, it had taken her days to find this outfit. She thought it was most suited the situation, maybe the hat was a bit over the top but she thought she looked lovely, much better than Mickie.

Olivia notice that Mickie kept her eyes out the window, she hadn't once looked her way throughout Dolly's dressing down, she would make a bet Mickie put Dolly up to it, the old bird wouldn't have thought of it on her own. How she hated Mickie Sullivan.

She tried to laugh it off, "Don't be silly Blake I've been wearing heels this high since I was a child."

"Still I have seen reports that say wearing those sorts of foot wear distorts your back and can give you all sorts of problems."

"I have never had a problem and my posture is perfect." She stated.

Thankfully the limo pulled into the driveway ending the conversation.

CHAPTER 29

A S SOON AS the vehicle stopped Mickie opened the door closest to her and got out, Blake helped Dolly out and was about to walk off when Olivia called, "Blake darling, can you give me a hand?" she held out her hand waiting for him to take it. Once she was out she laced her arm through his and said, "You can escort me in seeing you were so worried about me and my shoes." The look she gave Mickie that was one of the 'Cat getting the cream'.

Mickie helped Dolly into the mansion through the front doors; all the other guests were escorted around the side of the house to where the marquees were set up with food and drinks.

Mickie wasn't in the mood to mix with the other guest besides they were mostly Cybil's cronies she was happy to let Olivia entertain them. Mickie, she was content to stay in the kitchen with Dolly and have a cup of tea. Dolly was watching Olivia flit from guest to guest like she was the lady of the house, it should be Mickie out there but then again her Mickie was the complete opposite to that she-devil. Dolly watched as Mickie interacted with her granddaughter, if there was ever a girl born to have a house full of kids it was Mickie. She was so like her Mother it brought a tear to her eyes; she dearly hoped that Blake and Mickie could work out their problems and become a family again.

Just them Olivia burst into the kitchen making every one jump with the force in which she opened the door.

Looking at Dolly she said, "We need more trays of food outside, you're not paid to stand around talking." Olivia was about to turn around and walk away when Mickie stopped her.

"Who do you think you're talking to? You want more food talk to the caterers, Dolly's here as a member of the family and don't you ever speak to her like that again." Mickie was furious.

Olivia returned saying, "I'll speak to the hired help however I like and when I move in she will be the first thing to go."

Mickie laughed, "I feel sorry for you Olivia if you think you will ever live in this house."

This infuriated Olivia, "Really, you think you know everything. Well I will let you in on a secret Blake has just asked me to marry him and I said yes."

This time it was Dolly who spoke, "Girl it's a sin to tell lies you will go to hell for that. Blake would no sooner ask you to marry him than grow wings and fly."

Mickie was still laughing, "Oh Olivia you really must be desperate. I know that Blake hasn't asked you to marry him." Olivia opened her mouth to refute it but Mickie continued.

"Firstly he doesn't even like you and secondly he's already married."

By this time people close by could hear the raised voices or at least Olivia's high pitched screech and were turning towards the kitchen.

Olivia started towards Mickie, her eyes murderous, "You're a lying bitch Sullivan and you're deluding yourself if you think you are still married to Blake, and Cybil told me he divorced you."

Mickie smiled, "Sorry to burst your fantasy bubble but she failed miserably we are still very much married."

Olivia could see her future falling apart in front of her eyes; she would not lose everything to this bitch again.

As she reached out to grab Mickie Dolly stepped between them, Olivia shoved her so hard Dolly hit the floor with a thud, she yelped as the bone in her wrist snapped. Olivia was just about to put the boot in when Mickie grabbed her arm swinging her around, pulling her arm back she slammed her fist into Olivia's face connecting with her nose. Olivia went down like a sack of potatoes screaming so loud it hurt your ears. Mickie rushed to Dolly's side, she was holding her injured wrist and by the look on her face she was going into shock.

Blake and Richard rushed into the kitchen to see three women on the floor. Richard was the first to ask, "What the hell is going on?"

Olivia was holding her broken bleeding nose, "I want her arrested." Pointing to Mickie, "She broke my nose."

Richard grabbed the phone and called an ambulance.

Blake knelt down beside Dolly, he could see she was in pain and asked Mickie, "Want to tell me what happened?"

Mickie shrugged her shoulders, "Olivia pushed Dolly to the floor and broke her wrist, she was about to put the boot in, so I stop her from attacking hurt Dolly again."

Blake smiled, Mickie was such a tiny little thing no-one would credit her with attacking anyone let alone breaking someone's nose. "Did you hurt your hand?" Mickie shook her head smiling a little.

He turned around to see that someone had given Olivia and ice pack to put on her face.

Olivia was wailing like a banshee so much Richard yelled, "For Christ sake Olivia shut that god awful noise up."

The kitchen grew silent thank goodness, Richard then asked, "So is someone going to explain why there are two women injured in my kitchen?" He looked at Mickie?"

"Olivia stormed in here demanding Dolly get more trays of food when I told her Dolly was a guest and not to speak to her like that she went ballistic. Said that Blake had asked her to marry him and that when she moved in here Dolly would be thrown out. When I informed her we were still married she tried to attack me but Dolly got between us. Olivia threw her to the ground breaking her wrist, she was about to start kicking her when I pulled her away and stopped her."

Richard covered the smile forming with his hand; Olivia was a good foot taller than Mickie especially in those heels he was impressed she managed to find her target.

Before he could say anything Olivia screamed, "She lying! It was an unprovoked attack. The silly woman slipped I never laid a hand on her, she," pointing to Mickie, "Just grabbed me and started throwing punches." Olivia looked up at Blake innocently, "I did not tell her you had proposed to me I don't know where she got from. She just made that up to cause trouble between us. She has always been jealous of our close relationship Blake; seriously I think the girl has mental issues."

Blake couldn't believe Olivia was trying to blame everything on Mickie,

"Olivia I think you're the one with the issues, Mother would be proud. The fake tears, the indignation, putting all the blame on everyone else but you, really you should be an actress. Someone more gullible than I might have believed you except Father and I and the rest of our guests were standing right outside the kitchen window and heard the whole thing."

Olivia could have screamed; Cybil had been right, anything to do with Mickie Richard and Blake were blind, she always came out smelling like roses.

It was then the paramedics arrived and attended the injured parties, as they lifted Olivia on to the stretcher Richard approached her.

"Miss James your services will no longer be required at Cybil's office. Also I will be getting a restraining order against you for your assault on Dolly as well as Mickie, I will also be encouraging Dolly to press charges of assault, if you come anywhere near my family again I will have you arrested and locked up, do you understand?"

Olivia mumbled something that sounded like a 'Yes' from under her oxygen mask and was then carried to the waiting ambulance. This was far from over; Mickie Sullivan would not take Blake from her again.

Richard's driver took Dolly to the hospital to have her arm set.

That signalled the end of the wake, guest started to leave, most were disgusted in Olivia's behaviour, many were considering their future involvement with Olivia James. Within the hour the place was empty except for the cleaning crew.

Blake and Mickie went to pick Dylan up from Kathie's and took him back to the house where Richard was cooking tea.

Blake had been dying to ask Mickie, "So Mickie where did you learn to box?"

Mickie laughed, "I haven't. When you left your Mum got pretty hostile towards me, more than usual. Rick and Mike thought it a good Idea that I learn how to defend myself so Mike taught me some moves to get me out of trouble. He showed me where there were some vulnerable spots that didn't need a lot of effort to render someone incapacitated at least long enough for me to get away. Until today I have never had to use them. Blake I would never have used them on your Mother but I would have been able to stop her hurting me." She wanted to assure them she would never have physically hurt Cybil even while defending herself.

"I know Mickie even if my Mother did deserve it." Blake assured her.

Richard chipped in, "Well Honey I'm impressed she had a foot on you and you were still able to smack her."

"I didn't mean to break her nose; it was just a lucky shot." She said embarrassed she didn't believe in violence.

"Well at least I won't worry about you as much now that I know you have a mean right hook." Blake smiled.

"Sadly all it means is she is going to carry on Cybil's vendetta and be a pain in my side for the rest of my life."

Richard assured Mickie, "I meant what I said about the restraining order, I'll get Donald on to it first thing in the morning don't forget there were plenty of witness to verify your side of the story."

"I know but with Cybil gone I thought I might be able to breathe easier, Olivia has a lot of friends that could make my life a misery."

Blake held her hand, "Olivia won't be a problem and neither will her friends, the Hunter name still carries some weight in this town. Plus I think everyone saw Olivia's for what she really is. A lot of Mother's friends were disgusted not only because of her outfit but her attack on Dolly and trying to put the blame on you, she may not have as many friends as she thinks."

"I hope so, life was bad enough with Cybil's hatred I don't need half the town nipping at my heels I would sooner sell up and move."

"Sweetheart you might be surprised at the support you have got, not just for attending Cybil's funeral with grace and respect but for protecting Dolly." Richard stated.

"How is Dolly doing?" she asked

"Luckily it was a clean break; she'll be in plaster for six weeks but should mend well." Richard checked his watch.

"I think I will head home. Are you coming Blake?" Richard asked.

"Not yet Dad, if it's alright with Mickie we have some things we need to talk over, I'll catch a cab home." Blake answered.

Mickie could see Richard was unsure, "It's ok Rick you go on."

"OK then, will see you later Sweetheart." He leant over and kissed her cheek, then headed for home.

CHAPTER 30

MICKIE COLLECTED THEIR coffee cups and took them to the kitchen turning she found Blake leaning against the dining room table.

"So what did you want to talk about?" She asked

"Well you know how well we got on up at the cabin?" She nodded.

"I was thinking we might be able to make that a more permanent arrangement?" He watched her face intently.

"Don't you think it's a little soon?" She wanted him to be sure this time as there wouldn't be any chance for him to walk away like before.

"Not for me. I know I have a lot of trust to build with you Mickie but believe me I will never walk away again. I'm in this till the end of time. I want to watch our son grow into a man and bounce our grandchildren on my knee with you beside all the way. Mickie those years without you have been hollow and dark, there was no light, no sunshine, no rainbows.

Being with you this last week hearing your laughter seeing your smile has only made me realise what a fool I had been to leave you."

He walked over to her, reaching for her left hand. It was now or never. Taking a deep breath he got on one knee and asked, "Mickie Sullivan will you do me the greatest honour of marrying me and being my wife?" He reached into his pocket and pulled out the one karat golden diamond ring he had been carrying for days.

Mickie's eyes filled with tears, she had never stopped loving Blake even when he walked out all those years ago, even though she reasoned to herself it was something he had to do to find out what his heart truly wanted.

The ring he had bought her was gorgeous and she bet it would fit her finger perfectly. Still she hesitated. If he walked out on her again it would be kinder to shoot her dead.

He could see she still had some doubts. "I swear to you Mickie I will never hurt you like that again. To tell you the truth I need you far more than you will ever need me. I have seen the world without you in it and it is sad, cold, dark and miserable, it's a world I don't want to live in ever again.

She could see the sincerity on his face and hear it in his voice; he was being completely honest so she would be too.

"Blake you have to be one hundred percent positive it's what you want because it won't just be my life you tear apart it will also be Dylan's."

"Yes Mickie it's all and everything I want. I want us to be a family and maybe later add a little girl to the mix. I swear on everything I hold precious I will never leave you or our son again."

Tears rolled down her cheeks, "Then yes Blake Hunter I would love to be your wife."

He place the ring on her finger, it fit perfectly. He stood up pulling her into his arms. "You have made me the happiest man on this earth."

Looking up into his eye she noticed they too held a tear, he leaned down and kissed her showing her with his mouth how much he loved her.

CHAPTER 31

BLAKE NEVER CAUGHT that cab home. They were up bright and early the next morning to tell Dylan of their news. Mickie was a little nervous about telling him Blake was his father and that they were getting married again.

Dj took it in his stride he was excited about having a Dad and that he was going to be the 'Best Man' at their wedding. When Kathy came to pick him up he didn't even say goodbye before he was out the door telling everyone that his Dad was back and they were going to get married again cos the first one had run out. Kathie was very impressed and motioned she would call Mickie later for the details.

They cleaned up the breakfast dishes and headed to the boutique. When they arrived they noticed someone had covered the rear wall of the shop with graffiti. Mickie heart sank Tibbs was back again.

Blake searched the area before exiting the car and opened the back door ushering Mickie inside as quickly as possible, she went straight for the phone and called the police and Mike.

Mike and the detectives arrived at the same time, Mike headed for the dvr to watch the footage. There was Tibbs in living colour spray painting the rear of the shop. Somehow he must have found out Mickie was still alive. Mike was pissed turning to the officers he said, "I thought you said Tibbs would be removed from the area?"

"That's what the guys from OCU said." One of the detectives made a call.

Minutes later he said, "Tibbs rolled on his boss and they picked him up a week ago but seems someone let Barry walk out the door, they were so chuffed they got the head of the ring everyone miss Barry slipping away."

"Nice of them to keep us informed." Mike was angry. He got on the phone and ordered a detail to go to Mickie's house and another to the shop, he also sent an officer to Dylan's school just to be on the safe side. Mickie would have twenty four hour protection until this idiot was caught.

Tibbs took a nostril full of coke he couldn't believe his luck being able to walk out that station undetected. He was pissy when he heard that bitch survive the explosion but hell it just gave him another chance to get her. This time he would take her and have a bit of fun, she was one hot piece of ass and it had been a long time since he bedded such a beautiful woman better yet he would kill her while he was doing her. His excitement rose he was as getting a boner just thinking about it. It would have to happen soon though as he needed to get away from here before they caught him again. After another snort and he passed out on the flea bitten bed dreaming of Mickie.

Kyle ran into Olivia as she was leaving the hospital, she looked a mess.

Her nose had been bandaged and there were dark bruising around her eyes, Mickie had done a hell of a job, his lips twitched. He had never liked Olivia she was always looking out for the next sap to bleed dry he was glad their paths didn't cross very often.

"Ms James," he greeted her and was going to walk straight by when she grabbed his arm to halt his progress.

"Kyle? May I call you Kyle? You're Mickie's boyfriend aren't you?"

"What can I do for you Ms. James?" He enquired extracting her hand.

"I think you should take Mickie and her bra… boy and leave town."

"And why should I do that?" He gave her an irritated look, he was sure Olivia wasn't running on all cylinders.

"Blake Hunter is mine and I will do whatever it takes to make it so." She stated boldly.

"You are aware that he and Mickie are still married?" When Kyle over heard Mickie informing Olivia of that at the Cybil's Wake he knew he didn't stand a chance of winning her over.

Olivia waved her hand around, "That's just a mere technicality if indeed it's even the truth."

Kyle laughed, "I have known Mickie a long time and she is incapable of telling a lie so if she said she is still married then she is. I don't know what you think I can do for you Ms James but if it involves Mickie getting hurt in any way shape or form you can count me out."

Olivia was getting angry, "God you're not another one of her doting drooling saps. What is it with you men, you all hover around her like bees to honey she is just another scank who will spread her legs for someone that had the most money."

Now Kyle was getting snaky, "The only 'Scank' as you put it Ms James is you. You could never come close to being half the lady Mickie is and you never will. You have the morals of an alley cat. You strut around town with your nose in the air scorning those you think are below you, when in fact you are lower than a snake's belly. Your only claim to fame is that your parents had money"

She spluttered at his attack, "How dare you. Who do you think you are?

I come from one of the wealthiest family in the district and I have some very influential friends in this town Mr Anderson and you might like to remember I can make your life very difficult if I wish."

Kyle laughed, "Good thing your parents aren't alive to see you, they would be terribly disappointed in how you turned out Ms James and you might be surprised at how many friends you don't have. Your little tantrum at the Hunter Wake showed your true colours and opened the eyes of many people, I think you will find a lot of your so called 'Influential Friends' won't be taking your calls anytime soon. And before you start throwing threats around, I too have some influence in this town probably a lot more than you, so if I were you I would tread very carefully Ms James on whose life you think you can cause trouble with."

Olivia realised too late that she had over stepped the mark she started back peddling. "You will have to excurse my behaviour at the moment I'm not at my best and I'm taking a considerable amount of drugs that I rattle when I walk. You misunderstood me Kyle I have no intentions of hurting Mickie I am just letting you know that I intend to marry Blake Hunter and it would be kinder to Mickie if she wasn't here to see that. I know you two have a close relationship and thought you might like to help her out by taking her away."

Kyle couldn't believe the gall of this woman. "Ms James what makes you think Hunter would marry you even if he wasn't already married to Mickie?"

"Well I have a secret that will guarantee he will marry me."

She had a smug look on her face.

"And that would be?" He was curious to find out what she had on Hunter.

"Why I'm pregnant with his child. I know Blake he would not allow a child of his to be born out of wedlock. So you see it would be kinder for Mickie not to be here when the news gets out."

Sceptically he asked, "Really how far along are you?" As he could see no evidence on her extremely thin frame unless she was in the very early stages of pregnancy.

"Nearly four months so I'm going to start showing soon and if we are to be married before the birth it will have to happen in the next few months.

Kyle knew she had a screw loose now. Firstly there was no way she was four months pregnant and secondly Hunter had only been in town three months so if she was in fact pregnant which he thought was highly unlikely, it was someone else's. Thirdly if she was truly pregnant with Hunter's child she would have been shouting it from the roof tops the minute she knew just to rub it in Mickie's face.

Well Ms James I wish you all the best in your endeavour." Before she could say another word he walked off.

Olivia was so pleased with herself at how easily she had convinced Kyle that she was pregnant with Blake child, if he believed her others certainly would. Now all she had to do is put a bit of padding in her clothes so people would think her waist was expanding then she would demand Blake marry her. Shortly after they were married she would have a fall and lose the baby. Her future did not have children in it, that's why she had hoped to convinced Kyle to take Mickie, her brat and leave. She was getting excited just at the thought. She needed to go shopping for some bridal wear.

CHAPTER 32

THE POLICE PUT out an A.P.B. (All points Bulletin) on Barry Tibbs, they raided his usual haunts and his dealers but no one had seen Barry since he was first arrested. He had gone underground lying low until things cooled down a bit. Mike wasn't satisfied with what he called the police's "Lack of Concern"; they had got their man and didn't seem all that worried that Tibbs had got away, so he put his own people onto it. Mike knew Tibbs's type he had been gotten the better of by not only one but two women he wouldn't let that slight go. Mickie knew better than to argue when Mike told her what he had put into place but Mike couldn't talk her out of closing the shop, Blake assured him he would be with her at all the times, this eased some of Mikes apprehension plus he would have a team situated around the shop precinct. It was decided Dylan wouldn't attend school as it was too big an environment not only keep him but the other students and teachers safe as well, knowing Tibbs could get his hands on explosives they need to be doubly careful. Dj would go to work with his grandfather and have a tutor teach him for the time being.

Richard agreed and sourced a tutor he would set up a desk in his office so that he could also watch over Dylan.

The rest of the week went by uneventful except for several of Mickie's customers parading around in her sexy lingerie asking Blake for his opinion. She had never seen him blush before and by the end of the week he was spending most of his time in the office.

Several weeks went by when Mickie received a package in the mail, when she opened it several photographs fell out. They were scenes of a man and a woman having sex, she recognised the woman immediately as Olivia James the male was fuzzy and out of focus but he had the same build and dark hair as Blake. The note a companioning the photo said,

> *"I told you he was mine, this is to prove to you I wasn't lying. The best thing for you to do is divorce him and leave this town; he will never be faithful to you as these pictures show. Oh I nearly forgot I'm also pregnant with Blake's child. Do the right thing and take your child and leave."*

There was no signature there didn't need one she knew who had sent it. Mickie studied the photographs, they looked liked someone had deliberately tried to smudge the features of the male. While she was looking them over Blake entered the office carrying two cups of coffee.

"What are those?" He pointed to the photos.

"Well someone wants me to believe they are of you and Olivia James having sex."

Blake spat his coffee across the room, "What? Are you serious?"

She nodded and handed them to him.

One glance he knew they had been photo shopped, "Mickie you know this isn't me don't you?"

She thought she'd let him squirm for a minute.

"Well that person does have your build and hair colour."

"Mickie I swear to you on my life I never touched Olivia let alone slept with her."

She couldn't watch him suffer anymore, "its okay Blake I know it's not you, if it was I'm sure your face would be splattered all over the photo, I think you should read the note that came with it." She handed him the piece of paper.

He was ropable when he finished reading the note, "That bitch, how dare she."

It was then that Richard walked in one look at his son's face told him something was wrong. "What's the matter and who's the bitch?"

Blake handed him the note and photos. "Dad I want that woman locked up and the key thrown away."

Richard read the note, looked at the photos and agreed something needed to be done with Olivia James. He put made a call to Don, his lawyer.

He explained to Don what had happened, "Don I want her prosecuted to the full letter of the law. The woman is unstable and whatever needs to be done I want it done quickly she has caused enough problems for my family."

Don agreed to move on it immediately.

Richard asked Mickie, "Sweetheart you know this isn't Blake?"

Mickie smiled, "Yes Rick I know. If it was his face it wouldn't be fuzzy and out of focus plus I would have seen it long before now."

It seemed to be a day for visitors, Kyle knocked on the office door.

Mickie greeted him with a smile and hug.

"Hey stranger where have you been?" she asked.

He returned her embrace, "Conference interstate. Mickie is there somewhere we can talk?"

She looked a little confused then Blake spoke, "Anything you have to say to Mickie can be said in front of us all."

She nodded "What's it about Kyle?" she asked.

He looked at both men then shrugged his shoulders. "I ran into Olivia James before I left, she informed me that she has it in for you and Hunter."

"That's nothing new the whole town knows that" Mickie wonder what Olivia was up to by telling Kyle that.

"She told me to take you and DJ and leave town and that she was four months pregnant with Hunter's child."

"When was this? Blake asked.

"About a week ago just after Cybil's funeral. I was visiting a friend in the hospital when she was coming out."

Blake asked, "Why would she ask you to take Mickie away?"

"Don't know probably because I'm Mickie's friend. She tried to threaten me, said if I didn't do it she would ruin my business."

"Oh Kyle I'm so sorry." Mickie apologised.

"Sweetheart you have nothing to be sorry for, that woman is clearly not right in the head I just thought you should know."

Mickie hugged Kyle she was so sorry that Olivia had involved him in this mess. "Kyle I really am sorry for all of this. Richard is seeking legal advice on how we can stop her for doing this but it will take time."

Kyle returned her embrace, "Its ok Sweetheart there is nothing that crazy woman can do to me. I've also contacted my legal team and they are on to it hopefully they will lock her up and throw away the key."

Mickie laughed, "You and Blake have the same idea."

As it was close to the end of the day Mickies decided to close early it was decided that they would all go out for a meal. Mike's men collected Dylan and bought him to the shop and everyone left from there. Mike's men set up inside and a perimeter around the store in case Tibbs came back for another go.

CHAPTER 33

IT HAD BEEN almost a month since Tibbs's attack on the boutique, Mickie thought he may have finally given up and moved on, she had convinced Mike to reduce his security team as Blake was still attending the shop with her every day.

As there had been no sightings or any further disturbances from Tibbs Mike grudgingly agreed but he did keep the crew on her home.

It was the following week that both Mickie and Blake got a surprise when Olivia strolled in. She obviously had some surgery done in fact she had altered her appearance to the point of looking exactly like Mickie; she was also very much pregnant. Mickie thought her belly looking a little off kilter and was sure she was wearing some kind of prosthesis. Thankfully there were no customers in the shop at the time as Mickie knew that this was about to get ugly. Blake stayed in the office to hear what she had to say.

Olivia walked up to the counter rubbing her hand over her bump emphasizing it's size and asked, "Where's Blake?"

"He's busy. What do you want Olivia?"

"Who do you think I want, Blake of course? You do know I'm carrying his child." She continued to rub her stomach.

"Really Olivia I find that highly unlikely and what have you done to your face?"

Olivia brushed her hair back, "Nothing really just a tweak here and there, you should consider it yourself Mickie, keep the ravages of time away."

"Are you serious you could be my twin sister, for god sake Olivia why would you do that to yourself?"

"Isn't it obvious? Blake has a thing for you, as does every male over the age of ten so if I look more like you then he will want to be with me."

Mickie felt very sorry for Olivia but she was well and truly over her jealousy and machinations.

"Kyle told me you said you were four months pregnant that would make you about five months now, correct?

Olivia nodded, smiling smugly

"Well that's amazing as Blake has only been in town for four months and at least six of those weeks he was with me and our son. So if you really are pregnant which I sincerely doubt, then some other person is the father. You really should have done the math Olivia and made sure you had spent adequate time alone with Blake to give credence to your lies."

Olivia was fuming, "You have no idea how much time we spent together and in fact it only takes one shot, so to speak." She added crudely. "Mickie, it really doesn't matter if I am pregnant or not when word gets around that Blake has cast me and his unborn child aside he will lose a lot of respect and because of his crass and uncaring treatment I lose the baby this town will turn their backs on him and his family."

Mickie couldn't believe the lengths she would go to have Blake.

It was here that Blake picked up the phone and organised for a D.N.A. test to be conducted within the hour he would put an end to this debacle right now.

Mickie tried to get Olivia to understand Blake would not be with her. "Look Olivia you need to come to terms with the fact that Blake will never be with you even if you were legitimately pregnant with his child. He is married to me and we have no intentions of getting a divorce. Your so called affair is wholly and solely in your mind, you seem to be suffering the same affliction as his mother did and you know how that ended."

"How dare you," she screamed losing what little hold on reality she had. "Cybil was ten times the woman you will ever be and YOU were the one who drive her crazy if that's what she was. You're a witch casting your spell on the Hunter men sleeping with not only her son but her husband as well as every other man with money, they fall all over themselves to be near you, and you should be burnt at the stake like in olden times." By this time Olivia's voice had risen to a high pitch screech Blake thought it was time he stepped in.

Blake opened the office the door, "That's quite enough Olivia."

Olivia gasped, "Blake I didn't realise you were here, darling I've been trying to get hold of you for weeks."

"So it would seem to what purpose?" He asked.

"To tell you I'm having your child of course." She purred.

He pointed to her stomach, "So you're saying that is my child?"

She nodded pleased that he thought she was carrying his child.

"Right then I have organised to have a D.N.A. test done today." When she tried to refuse, he quickly cut her off. "You can't refuse Olivia especially since you have been running around this town shooting your mouth off saying the baby is mine now you have the chance to prove it. We both know what the outcome will be it will prove without any shadow of a doubt that it's not mine and you're a liar."

Olivia went ballistic then just as Mike was coming through the door; he pulled out his phone and called the police.

"You two think you are so smart." All the while she was screaming at them she was trying to tear the prosthesis from her body.

"I will destroy both you and your Father Blake and as for you Sullivan, You'd better watch your back because I'm going to get you for ruining everything I have ever wanted, for killing the only Mother I ever loved, for turning the only man I ever loved against me. You better keep your eyes open because you will never see me coming but you will feel the knife I plunge deep into you evil black heart." Olivia was about to storm out when she turned and fell into the arms of a waiting police officer.

Righting herself she said, "What the hell are you doing? Let me go you moron." She screamed at the officer as he placed her in handcuffs.

The officer addressed Olivia, "Miss James you need to come with me we will get this all sorted out. The officer nodded to Blake and Mickie and thanked Mike on his way out.

Blake asked Mickie, "You ok Sweetheart?" He put his arm around her.

Mickie was shaking what was wrong with people in this town.

"Yes but that woman needs some serious help. Why would someone change their whole appearance, to become someone else just to get a man? God Blake it's just like your mother all over again. Maybe I should move away at least I'd have some peace."

Mike could understand where Mickie was coming from, for almost ten years she had been given grief by Cybil, Olivia and their cronies in one way or another and now Tibbs was added to the mix.

"Sweetheart let Don sort her out, why don't we close up and call it a day?"

Mickie nodded she was just over it all. What she wanted was a long soak in a bath and a relaxing massage.

CHAPTER 34

THEY PICKED DJ up on the way and grabbed some takeout they eat as soon as they got home. After dinner Mickie left the boys to their "Man talk" and headed for her bath.

She had been soaking for nearly half an hour when Blake knocked on the door, he entered. The room had a mystical feel about it; scented candle filled the air with sensual aroma, their flickered light in the steamy atmosphere giving the room an eerie look like you were walking into thick fog, soft music coming from her iPod. Mickie was lying submerged in a bubble negligee, her long hair dangling over the edge of the bath; she looked peaceful and incredibly sexy. He loved her so much he though his heart would explode, he had been such a fool to walk away from her all those years ago.

He crept over to the side of the bath and sat on the edge just happy watching her.

"Are you going to sit there all night or are you going to join me?"

A voice thick, sultry and inviting urged him on.

He didn't need her asking twice, his clothes were off in less than thirty seconds, she had moved over to make room for him. The water level rising as he settled into the bath.

"Where's Dj?" she asked

"Fast asleep so the rest of the night is ours." He smiled think of all the things he wanted to do to her. He took hold of her leg and massaged the balls of foot, she moaned in pleasure. He worked his way to her carves then to her thigh all the while pleasurable sounds telling him how much she was enjoying his attention.

He then started on the other leg giving it the same treatment, when he had finished he stood up and moved behind her. She felt his erection pressing into her back as he settled behind her he was as hard as a rock.

He slowly massaged her neck, shoulders and worked his way down her arms. Her nipples had swollen to hard buds screamed for his attention but still he took his time. He gradually worked his way down to her breasts, tenderly and lovingly caressing them, when he gently squeezed her nipples she thought she would explode. Her writhing was sending cascades of water over the sides but she didn't care all she wanted was Blake's hands on the body. He lifted her up resting her on his legs so he could reach further down her body to her core. He barely touched her and she exploded in ecstasy, pushing her bottom against his manhood was nearly his undoing.

Whispering in her ear he said, "Sweetheart how about we take this to the bedroom?"

She nodded. He lifted her out of the water wrapping her in a bath towel and carried her to the bedroom, laying her on the bed. She was so utterly beautiful all she had on was a smile that lit up the room.

He softly said, "Roll over babe." He grabbed the moisturizing lotion off the dresser.

Pouring some into his hand to warm it slightly he gently rubbed it down her back massaging her neck, shoulders, ribs and buttocks, working his way down her legs to her feet when he had finished he said, "Roll over." Again he filled his hand with the sweet smelling cream, starting with her hands working his way up to the shoulders and neck.

Mickie was in as much agony as pleasure her whole body was on fire for his touch, his fingers were everywhere except her most intimate spots and they were screaming for his attention, is was sheer torture. The pleasure from the massage was intense but his bypassing her breasts and pelvic area was absolute agony. He could see she was enjoying his touch and the disappointment when he skirted her breasts, this was her night, he wanted to make it last and he knew the minute he touched her there would be no holding back.

Enough was enough she begged, "Blake please."

Finally he cupped her womanhood, she start to shake. He rubbed his thumb over her sensitive nub her moans were music to his ears. He gently inserted a finger into her moist, throbbing passage; her muscles gripped his finger tightly, moving slowly at first back and forth her body pushed against his hand. He leant over sucking a hardened nipple into his mouth one tug was all it needed and she exploded gyrating against his hand as her orgasm over took her wave after wave of ecstasy.

It had been so long since she had been intimate with a man her orgasms were almost painful, still he hadn't finished with her. He drew her other nipple into his mouth sucking a little harder Mickie couldn't believe her body reacted so quickly after such a powerful orgasm. She needed to rest for a moment and give him some of the same treatment.

She cupped his head bringing his mouth up to hers, kissing him passionately; she rolled over on top of him. Moving from his lips she kissed his neck slowly moving down his body, she licked his nipples his groan of pleasure urging her on. Nibbling her way down his abdomen to his apex, gently she encircled his manhood it was as hard as granite and as smooth a marble, a moisture bubble glistened the top she couldn't help herself opening her mouth she licked it off. Blake knew he was close to the edge if he felt her mouth on him it was all over.

"Sweetheart if you keep that up it's going to be over before we start." He pleaded.

She ignored his plea and engulfed his silken shaft with her hot mouth gently squeezing his balls as she wrapped her tongue around him sucking hard, that did it Blake exploded in her mouth, she greedily took what he offered. He had never come so hard in all his life his body was shaking from the effect.

He pulled her up his body to lie on top of him, "Baby I wanted to do so much to you but after that I'm depleted." He apologised.

She laughed, "Why do you think I did it? I haven't had that many orgasms since you left and I think if I had one more it would have crippled me in."

Blake frowned if he understood her right she hadn't been with anyone since he left, "Mickie are you saying you haven't been with anyone else?"

She looked into his eyes, "Blake I always thought you would come back and then when you didn't I had Dylan to think of as well as building a business sex didn't have a high priority in my life. I will admit if you hadn't come home when you did I was seriously thinking of dating again, Dj needs a male figure in his life, Richard is great but I was thinking more along the lines of someone being there on a daily basis."

If they were going to have a fresh start he needed to tell her the truth.

"Mickie," he started.

She could see by the look on his face that he was going to tell her he had been with other women, even though it hurt to know she understood somehow.

"I have something to tell you." He didn't want to hurt her but he knew it would.

She could see how difficult it was for him so she made it easier.

"You've been with other women?"

He wouldn't lie, "Yes. To be truthful and I know it's terrible but they were only one night stands, not even the night really and only after I got the divorce papers. I went a little crazy trying to forget you but it only made me realise what I was missing and that I was only using them. Dad said you have a close relationship with your accountant?"

She smiled when she heard a trace of jealousy in his voice, "Yes. I have attended a few events as Kyle's companion, he has proposed to me several times". Blake felt a twinge on the region of his heart.

"If you hadn't come back then I would have seriously looked at taking our relationship to the next level. He's a good man, has his own wealth so I know he wouldn't be marrying me for mine, he's great with Dylan and Richard likes him."

He wrapped her in his arms, "Then I'm glad I came back when I did. I'm so sorry for the hurt and pain I have caused you Sweetheart and if it takes me the rest of my life to prove how much I love and need you then I hope to live until I'm a hundred years old to show you."

"Blake I never stopped loving you. When the divorce papers came through I thought 'He will come to his senses' so until you did I just buried my feelings and concentrated on building my business and raising our son but you were cutting it fine I had just about given up six years is a long time."

God he had been such a fool. "Mickie I will make it up to you and Dylan I swear. This is where I want to be with my family and if at all possible to give Dylan and brother or sister sometime in the future."

She smiled and snuggled close to his body; she loved this man with all her heart and was glad he found his way back to her. "That would be wonderful." They slept the rest of the night embraced in each other's arms.

CHAPTER 35

TIBBS HAD HEARD from a snitch that the woman from underwear shop was at the police station, he had staked it out hoping to grab her. It would be a real coo to take her from right under the copper's nose. The door opened and she walked out, he followed her to the cab rank. As she went to enter he pushed her in and got in beside her.

"What the hell do you think you're doing, get out of my cab." Olivia screamed at Tibbs.

"Shut up bitch." He growled. To the cabby he said, "Corner of Thomas and Clayton Streets and make it quick."

Olivia not one to know when she was in real trouble said screamed, "Cab driver take me back to the police station I want this man arrested."

Tibbs pulled out his gun, "Bitch if you know what's good for you keep that mouth of your shut tight or I will shut it for you."

She opened her mouth unload a tirade of abuse at him when he back handed her splitting her lip. Now she was scared, blood dripped from her broken lip onto her lap she looked up at the rear view mirror hoping to catch the cab drivers eyes but he stared straight ahead. She tried to move closer to the door if they stopped at a set of lights she would try and jump out. Tibbs thought 'Miss Prim and Proper' might try to escape so he latched onto her arm with biting fingers she knew they would leave a bruise.

They were heading for the outskirts of town Olivia had never been this far out of the city, the dwellings were old and in various states of repair. The cab pulled up at the address given by the Tibbs, it was an old bank building, two story brick structure. The front windows had been boarded up, the local kids using to display their graffiti artwork.

Tibbs dragged her from the cab by the hair to the front door, the cabbie didn't hang around he took off screeching the tyres. Tibbs knew he didn't have much time, knew the cops would be on their way soon, he should have shot the driver, probably would have if the bitch hadn't been squirming so much.

He albeit threw Olivia through the door, stumbling she noticed a scruffy looking mattress and dirty blankets on the floor along with an array of drug paraphernalia, cigarette butts and discarded food packages.

"Get comfortable Toots this will be you home for a while." He sneered.

"Are you insane? Why have you brought me here? Do you know who I am?" Some of her anger was returning.

"Sure I know who you are, you're that 'smart ass bitch' that thought she could get away with ripping me off. First you let Rachael get away, then you try and stooge me by filling the bag with fake notes." He moved over to the table and took a snort of powder. "You know I thought I had you when you dropped off that money and I blew everything up but you must be like a cat and have more than one life, which is good cos you're gunna be needing them."

Olivia had no idea what this lunatic was talking about. "I have no idea what you are talking about. Maybe you have mistaken me for someone else?"

"No way sugar tits I would know you anywhere, been watching you for months. You like to have men around you don't you? Bowing and serving to your every needs, well this is one man that won't be kissing you feet in fact it will be you doing the kissing and it will be a lot more than my feet." He laughed.

Olivia had to find a way out of here and soon, but it seemed the front door was the only out as all the windows were covered and the stairway had seen better days. She would have to pick the right time probably when he was at his most venerable maybe when he went to sleep.

"You might as well stop that mouse running around your pretty head you ain't getting out of here anytime soon sweet cheeks. Why don't you come over here and make old Bazza a drink?" He pointed to the fridge and table that held several bottles of spirits. "You can make yourself one if you like."

Olivia didn't move.

Barry was getting angry, "Bitch, make me a drink now!" He let a shot off into the ceiling, plaster particles fell to the floor as she hurried over to the table. With shaking hands she poured him a drink. When she handed it to him he grabbed her arm pulling her onto his lap.

"Now how about you keep Bazza here happy and give him a little sugar?" He nuzzled her neck, what he thought was a quiver of excitement was instead of the squirm of revulsion she felt, he grabbed her breast squeezing it harshly, she pulled out of his clasp.

"Now don't be getting all prissy on me bitch you give it away pretty freely to those other guys now you can give me some of it unfortunately for you I won't be able to suck up and buy you a fancy dinner but I'm quite happy to share last night's leftovers with ya."

Olivia thought she would be sick, why was this happening to her?

She looked over at Tibbs and thought at one time he might have been a handsome man but drugs and his lifestyle had taken their toll on him. He looked gaunt and haggard, his hair was long and scraggy and he was in need of a bath and shave, something he probably hadn't had in months.

"I need to use the bathroom." She stated

"Sorry Honey you will have to squat on the floor." He mumbled

"I'm not using the floor, where is the bathroom?" she said, indignant.

"It's upstairs but don't blame me if you get hurt those stair could go at anytime." He snapped as he snorted more cocaine.

Olivia was hoping when she got back he would have passed out, the amount of drugs and alcohol he had consumed she was amazed he was still standing.

Meanwhile the cab driver had reported the kidnapping to the police and they were now on their way.

Olivia carefully made her way up the stairs she really didn't need the bathroom she just wanted to get as much distance as she could from Barry and see if she could find a way out of there. She searched the other rooms but they too had the windows boarded up and the doors screwed shut. Tears filled her eyes there was no escape, she just hoped the cab driver reported the incidence to the police.

Barry realised his companion had been going a long time, "Hey Princess you fallen down the hole?"

Olivia realised he would come look for her if she didn't go back so she made her way down the rickety staircase, while she had been gone he had been fantasizing about all the things he wanted to do to her. Barry was watching her every move and getting more excited the closer she got, she had a smoking hot body, big tits, long hair that he could pull while riding her from behind.

Olivia notice the lustful looks Barry was giving her, she regretted now not taking those self defence courses.

Barry gut up out of the chair and handed her a drink, he had added a little relaxant to hers, grabbing his own he said, "Have a seat and let's get to know each other."

He albeit pushed her into the couch, "Drink up Sweet cheeks let's be hospitable."

"Why have you taken me?" She said barely above a whisper.

Firstly there's the fact you wouldn't hand over Rachael, the lying scheming bitch, Secondly there were all those fake bills you tried to palm off on me and thirdly there was you not dying in the explosion, which I might add took me a full day to set up. Now the way I see it you owe me big time, so you can either repay it in blood or pussy, either's fine with me."

"So you're going to kill me?" She whispered.

Tibbs shrugged his shoulders, "More than likely, yes but not before you have paid back what you owe. If you're really good I might even reconsider the killing part."

Olivia knew she was going to die, if the police were coming they would have been here already. She started to cry why was this happening to her? She wasn't a bad person, selfish and arrogant yes but not bad.

"Now, now Princess no need to cry if you keep old Bazza here happy he will keep you around."

This guy was nuts, he kept referring to himself like a third person, she had no intentions of having sex with the lunatic, so had resigned herself to the fact she was going to die.

She tried to think of ways to delay the inevitable, "I'm hungry can you get us some food?"

Barry flipped open his phone and ordered pizza to be delivered, this would give her an opportunity to let the driver know she was in trouble.

Barry poured himself another drink and sat beside Olivia, "Now how about you finish your drink and you and me get to know each other a little better."

Olivia obeyed taking a large mouthful it tasted a little bitter but she swallowed it anyway anything to keep this guy happy until the delivery driver arrived. Again her encouraged her to drink, this time she finished the glass, Barry got up and refilled it again adding a little something to relax her.

Within half an hour Olivia was feeling the effects of the drug she could barely keep her eyes open, somewhere in her foggy mind it realised she had been drugged.

She tried to get up but fell straight back down, in a slurred, accusing voice she said, and "You drugged me."

"Nah just gave you something to relax."

Olivia realised she could barely move, that when Barry moved in. He started undoing the buttons on her blouse, she was powerless to stop him. Inch by inch he exposed her breasts to his greedy gaze, running his finger down her cleavage. She shuddered not in desire but revulsion Barry took it as a green light to continue. Olivia opened her mouth to scream but nothing came out, there was nothing she could do. She closed her eyes and cried until he had his fill of her. When he had finished he passed out on the floor, Olivia having gained some mobility dressed herself, she was making her way to the door when all of a sudden it was kicked in and men with guns drawn charged at her. She fell to the ground cover her head with her hands sobbing. A female voice finally penetrated her cloudy mind, "Ms James it's all right, your safe now."

Next paramedics where beside her lifting her up on to a gurney covering her in a blanket and strapping her in, wheeling her to the waiting ambulance.

Police had handcuffed Barry who was still unconscious another gurney was brought in for him, as they tried to load him into the same ambulance as Olivia she went hysterical, another one was called to transport Barry.

Olivia was the talk of the town, TV. and newspaper people were clamouring for an exclusive interview and for once in her life Olivia wished no-one knew her, the kidnapping and rape had done something truly terrible to her psyche as it would anyone who had suffered as she had. She demanded only a female doctor attend to her, would scream if a male entered her room Nightmares tortured her mind every night she barely slept, refused to take anything to help her sleep, eventually she stopped talking to everyone. The doctor recommended she be assessed by a psychiatrist and suggested she be transferred to 'Good Hope Sanatorium' where she would get the care she required.

Mickie and Blake were shocked to hear what happened to Olivia and that the perpetrator had been Barry Tibbs, he had obviously mistaken her for Mickie. Mickie felt terrible that she had been put through that and was now she was a patient of Good Hope, at least this way she would get the proper care she needed and hopefully come to terms with her feelings towards Mickie and Blake.

Now that Tibbs was once again in custody and because of the crimes he had committed while escaping custody meant he would not get any leverage on his sentencing, he would be going to prison for the rest of his life. If they were lucky he would put in the same one as his old boss and would be dealt with accordingly, either way he would never be a threat to Mickie or her family again.

Life resumed for the Hunter family, Mickie and Blake remarried three months after Tibbs's arrest and the following year they were blessed with twins one of each, Dylan wasn't too thrilled with having a baby sister but his little brother delighted him, Richard met up with Lucy Andrews, his high school sweetheart at a convention in the city and married her six months later.

Blake did eventually join the family firm but as Head of their I.T. department, Richard had semi retired and was happily taking time out to enjoy life, he and Lucy would often take Dj on trips with them and spend time at the cabin.

Mickie had leased her boutique to Rachael and was enjoying being a Mum to her kids something she missed with Dylan and being a wife to Blake, her life was wonderful and complete.

The End